I0610000

Anonymous

Memorial Sketch of Lafayette S. Foster

Anonymous

Memorial Sketch of Lafayette S. Foster

ISBN/EAN: 9783337154219

Printed in Europe, USA, Canada, Australia, Japan

Cover: Foto ©Raphael Reischuk / pixelio.de

More available books at **www.hansebooks.com**

MEMORIAL SKETCH

OF

LAFAYETTE S. FOSTER, LL.D.,

UNITED STATES SENATOR FROM CONNECTICUT, AND ACTING
VICE-PRESIDENT OF THE UNITED STATES.

FOR PRIVATE DISTRIBUTION.

BOSTON:
FRANKLIN PRESS: RAND, AVERY, & COMPANY.
1881.

PREFACE.

An exhaustive memoir of the late Senator Foster would properly include a detail of the secret history of the war for the Union, or at least a review of its leading events, with an analysis of the political occurrences which preceded it. Mr. Foster was so intimately connected with the administration of President Lincoln, that the story of his life would involve a narration of the history of the country during those stirring and eventful years. The statesmen who were most competent to detail the events of that period of the national administration and Mr. Foster's participation in it have, most of them, like the subject of our sketch, gone to their rest. The record has in a great degree perished with them. Mr. Foster was on many occasions in his later life urged to commit to manuscript his recollections of those days. He replied that he had thought at times of doing so, but that he had been prevented by too engrossing occupation with public business during those years when the details were most vivid to his recollection. He never afterward found the opportunity to write these chapters of his experience ; and the country has occasion to regret it, as a valuable leaf in her history is thus forever lost.

The record of Mr. Foster's beautiful private and social life is also necessarily imperfect. Personal recollectious of his geniality and wit are as evanescent as the occasions which called them forth. His personal and social qualities will remain with all who knew him intimately among their sweetest memories, but the complete record can only be found written in the hearts of those who loved him. It is not available for the printed page.

4

It is the object of this sketch, then, to preserve the outlines only, and salient features of Mr. Foster's public and private life. To it are appended such extracts from the records of the day, and comments from the public press, as serve to give completeness to certain details, and to illustrate more fully some features of Mr. Foster's life and character. It is hoped that the collection of these memorials may afford some gratification to those who loved our departed friend, and may serve in some degree to perpetuate the memory of an honorable and useful life.

W. H. W. C.

July, 1881.

MEMORIAL OF

LAFAYETTE S. FOSTER.

LAFAYETTE SABIN FOSTER was born in the town of Franklin, New London County, Conn., a part of the original town of Norwich, on the 22d of November, 1806. His parents were poor, but of high character, and greatly respected. His father, Capt. Daniel Foster, served with distinction in the war of the Revolution, taking part in the battles of White Plains, Stillwater, and Saratoga. In the last-named engagement he was a lieutenant in one of the Connecticut regiments (Col. Latimer's), and received his warrant of promotion to the post of adjutant while upon the field. Daniel Foster's father, Nathan Foster of Stafford, Conn., is believed to be identical with the Nathan Foster of Ipswich, Mass., who was a great grandson of Reginald Foster, who came to this country from England in the year 1638, tradition says, from Exeter. Daniel Foster's mother was Hannah Standish, a great granddaughter of Capt. Miles Standish, the famous colonial soldier.

Mr. Foster's mother was Welthea Ladd of Franklin, the second wife of Daniel Foster, to whom she was married in 1802. She was connected by lineage with some of the principal colonist families of eastern Connecticut. She was a woman of great energy and shrewdness, of more than common intellectual ability, and highly gifted in conversational power. Mr. Foster cherished a peculiarly tender affection for his mother, and his care for her and for his only sister throughout their lives was unceasing. During his early career he pressed upon his mother all she would receive of his limited earnings ; and it was a matter of pride with him, that, before he took possession of the beautiful home where he spent his later years, he had just provided for his mother a home equally well suited to her wishes. Mrs. Foster died Feb. 11, 1851, at the age of eighty-eight years, having been spared long enough to see in the brilliant career of her beloved son a realization of her fondest hopes. It is said by those who knew both Mr. Foster and his mother intimately that he strongly resembled her in some of his intellectual traits.

Of his father, who died Jan. 28, 1824, aged seventy-nine years, Mr. Foster's earliest recollections were of sitting upon his knee, and listening to stories of the march, the battle, and the camp. In an address delivered at the Burgoyne centennial celebration at Schuylerville, N.Y., on the 17th of October, 1877, Mr. Foster referred to those Revolutionary tales as having made an impression upon his mind too deep and vivid to be ever erased. He quoted from memory a stanza of a song which his father was in the habit of singing, especially on the 4th of July, a day which he never failed to celebrate. It ran as follows : —

> " The 17th of October,
> The morning being clear,
> Brave Gates unto his men did say,
> ' My boys, be of good cheer !
> For Burgoyne, he is advancing,
> And we will never fly ;
> But, to maintain our chartered rights,
> We'll fight until we die ! ' "

It may be that these stirring recitals of his father first awakened in his impressionable mind that intense pride in his native land which was so manifest on many occasions in Mr. Foster's after-life.

Mr. Foster's only inheritance from his parents and ancestry was an honored name and an unstained character. In preparing himself for active life his own resources were early called into requisition. His education was begun in the common schools of his native town. At the age of sixteen he entered upon his preparation for college under the tuition of the Rev. Abel Flint, D.D., of Hartford, with whom he studied for nine months. During the two subsequent winters he taught in the schools of his native town, being then a mere boy in years. In 1824 he completed his preparatory studies with the Rev. Cornelius B. Everest of Windham, and in February, 1825, entered Brown University at Providence, R.I., where he was graduated in September, 1828, with the highest honors of his class. While in college he was noted for his excellent scholarship, his tireless diligence, his remarkable memory, his ready wit, and his genial social qualities. The resolute industry of Mr. Foster in working his way through college without pecuniary assistance from his father or other friends, was one of the best manifestations of a conspicuous trait in his character, and an omen of his success in after-life.

After his graduation, Mr. Foster taught during the winter as an assistant in the school of Mr. Roswell C. Smith in Providence. In the following spring he began the study of the law at Norwich, Conn., in the office of Calvin Goddard, a member of the famous " Hartford Convention " and one of the leading lawyers of the State. In the autumn of 1829 he took charge of an academy at Centreville, Md.;

and during the year spent at that place he was admitted to the Maryland bar. Then, returning to his native State, he completed his law studies in the office of Judge Goddard, and at the November term of the court in 1831 was admitted to the bar of New London County. In 1833, at the solicitation of many friends, he opened a law office in Hampton, Windham County, but a year afterwards returned to Norwich, which became his home for life.

His early career as a lawyer was very successful, and he rose with rapidity to the position of a leader at the Norwich bar. He soon found himself chiefly engaged in the higher class of cases, in the entire eastern part of the State. His habit was to prosecute his cases with the utmost zeal and energy. As a pleader he was closely analytic in his arguments, earnest, serious, and persuasive. He obtained highly remunerative fees in many instances, but he was always ready to protect and assist a poor client without reward.

It was always characteristic of Mr. Foster, that, while he devoted himself with zeal and activity to furthering the interests of his clients, he was never anxious about, or greatly occupied with, his own financial affairs. This was especially true during the later years of his life, when he left the care of his important business interests very largely in the hands of his trusted friend and adviser, Mr. Frank Johnson of Norwich.

On the 2d of October, 1837, Mr. Foster was married to Joanna Boylston Lanman, daughter of the Hon. James Lanman of Norwich, who was a judge of the Supreme Court of Connecticut and a senator of the United States. Two daughters and a son were the fruit of this union, all of whom died at a very early age. Mrs. Foster died in April, 1859, after a brief illness, deeply lamented by the entire community of Norwich and by a large circle of friends elsewhere. These successive bereavements produced a profound effect upon the sensitive nature of Mr. Foster; and it required the utmost resources of a naturally strong character, with the consolations of an earnest Christian faith, to save him from utter prostration.

On the 4th of October, 1860, Mr. Foster was again married, to Martha Prince Lyman, daughter of the Hon. Jonathan Huntington Lyman of Northampton, Mass., who, although he died young, was one of the most eminent members of the bar of that State. Mrs. Foster survives her husband.

———————

At an early period of his professional life Mr. Foster took an active interest in politics, and his abilities and the earnestness of his opinions quickly brought him into prominence. In 1835 we find him editing "The Norwich Republican," a Whig journal; but he soon relinquished the position, owing to the rapid increase of his legal business. In the spring of 1839 he was chosen one of the representatives of the town of Norwich in the General Assembly of the State. This honor was repeated in the years 1840, 1846, 1847, 1848, 1854, and 1870. At once, upon his entry into the Legislature, he took an active part in the business of the committees and of the House. In his second term he appears among the foremost debaters of that body. Some of his speeches at this time display conspicuously the acuteness in argument, and the ironical humor, which marked his more important efforts in after-life.

In the year 1847 he was chosen speaker of the House of Representatives, and was re-elected in 1848. In 1848 he began to attract attention as a fitting man for the United States Senate. In the Whig Legislative caucus of that year he received several votes for the nomination to that high position, and in the subsequent balloting in the House he also commanded some support. In 1854 he was chosen Speaker for the third time. His address on taking the chair was brief, and so clearly illustrative of the man and his principles that it is here given in full. Mr. Foster said, —

"I thank you, gentlemen, for this expression of your respect and confidence. It shall be my endeavor to discharge the duties to which you have called me, with fidelity and impartiality.

"The love of order and decorum which has so uniformly characterized the General Assembly of our State, and which, I have no doubt, will be a prominent characteristic of this House, will render the duties of your presiding officer comparatively pleasant and of easy accomplishment.

"Our session commences at a period of unusual interest. The mightiest nations of the eastern continent are just entering upon a war, — a war to be waged with more of pomp and circumstance, and on a scale of more imposing grandeur, than any the world has yet seen. Our own country is agitated by a domestic question scarcely less exciting than war itself.

"These topics, it is true, do not fall directly within the pale of our legislation. It is fit, however, that our national government should take its tone and impress from the people and from the State governments. It is fit that the voice of Connecticut should be heard, and not altogether unheeded, in our national councils, declaring, as she does, with one accord, that our foreign policy is peace, — peace, as far more glorious than war; that our domestic policy, on such a question as now agitates our country, is liberty, — *liberty and right, not slavery and might.*

"We enter, I trust, on the duties before us, with entire respect and good-will towards each other individually, and as members of different parties. These feelings ought to increase. If the divine precept of doing as we would be done by could at once be adopted in politics, it might then prove as infallible a guide as it has been in morals.

"May a kind Providence be over us to counsel and direct us!"

On the 8th of June of that year, having been elected a senator of the United States, he resigned his office and his seat in the House. His fame as a presiding officer and parliamentarian has never been excelled, if equalled, by that of any of the other distinguished men of the State who have occupied that position. He uniformly exercised its duties in such a manner as to win the respect of members of all parties. A New Haven newspaper of that date, speaking of his resignation, remarked, " No gentleman in past years has retired from the same post of honor with more of the hearty esteem and good wishes of the Legislature than Mr. Foster." In a letter to a friend he writes: "I confess I like the duties and responsibilities of the position; even when the excitement is greatest and the rush most intense, it suits my taste and temper."

Previous to this, in the year 1846, Mr. Foster made his first journey to Europe. He sailed on the 7th of October for Liverpool in the packet ship " Henry Clay," Capt. Nye, and arrived home in the middle of December. His time was spent mostly in London and Paris. In the former city, aside from an eager search among the chief historical objects of interest, he was a diligent visitor in the law courts. The observations of men and places recorded in his brief diary are singularly acute. Though his journal was not minute, he brought from his travels a vast store of interesting recollections. His appreciation of rare and beautiful objects in nature and art was exceedingly keen; and his comments were made with freshness and simplicity, as well as with discriminating taste.

Later on, in 1850 and 1851, during the interval of his legislative membership, Mr. Foster was the candidate of the Whig party for governor of Connecticut. In both of these years there was no choice by the popular vote, and the General Assembly elected a Democratic governor. In 1851, although there was a small Whig majority in the House, there was a division in the ranks. Mr. Foster's opponent, Hon. Thomas H. Seymour, was elected by the close vote of a hundred and twenty-two to a hundred and twenty-one. Later in the same session an attempt was made to choose a United States senator. A number of ballots were taken. The Whigs vainly attempted to unite upon Hon. Roger S. Baldwin of New Haven, and afterwards upon Mr. Foster, both of whom came within half a dozen votes of an election. The Legislature finally adjourned without action; and the next House, being Democratic, sent the Hon. Isaac Toucey to the Senate.

In 1851 the degree of LL.D. was conferred upon Mr. Foster by Brown University. In the same year he was elected mayor of Norwich, to which office he was again chosen the following year, without one vote in opposition; a rare mark of confidence in a public man on the part of those who know him most intimately.

Mr. Foster was now in the prime of his manhood. At the bar of Connecticut he had attained a place among the foremost lawyers of the State. In the appendix will be found pen pictures of him as he appeared to his contemporaries during these years. He had also reached an eminent position as a leader of public opinion. He had been long opposed by conviction to the institution of slavery, and he shared the indignation which was so widely felt in the North at the political encroachments of the slaveholding interests. On a later public occasion he claimed an anti-slavery record as far back as 1836. Yet he was an ardent Whig, and regarded with disfavor the first efforts to institute a Free-Soil party. When, however, it became evident that nothing was to be hoped from either of the existing parties, Mr. Foster did not hesitate to sever his party ties, and became a member of the " Republican " organization from its beginning. In May, 1854, two days after the passage of the Kansas-Nebraska Bill by the national House of Representatives, he addressed a public meeting held in New Haven to denounce the measure. On this occasion he declared that the time for speech-making had passed, and the time for action had come. He pledged his efforts to whatever course of action was decided, after calm deliberation, to be the best. " Let us consult," he said, " and, whatever conclusion we arrive at, let us join heart and hand in carrying it into action."

On the 19th of May, 1854, Mr. Foster was elected to the United States Senate by the votes of the Whigs and Free-Soilers for the full term of six years. Hon. Francis Gillette of Hartford, Free-Soiler, was chosen at the same session

of the Legislature to fill the remainder of the term for which
Hon. Truman Smith, who had resigned, was elected. On
the 10th of May, 1860, Mr. Foster was returned to the
Senate for a second term of six years. A contemporary
Republican journal, referring to his senatorial services dur-
ing the first term, remarked as follows : —

"Senator Foster, during his present term in the Senate, has
represented the State with great dignity and ability. His courtesy
and calmness in the discussion of all topics have made him respected
by his political opponents in that body, and have won for him the
esteem of the Republican Congressmen. . . . It is a remarkable
fact, that, during the entire canvass, excited and bitter as it was,
our opponents, though regarding the senatorship as of more importance than any other matter, were not able to make any attack
whatever upon Mr. Foster, or to name an act or vote of his to which
reasonable objection could be taken. But the Republicans were
able to point with pride to his whole course in the Senate, and to
appeal to the people with great effect to save the State from the
disgrace of his defeat."

During the earlier portion of his senatorial service Mr.
Foster was not a frequent participator in debate. At this
period the most exciting questions before the Senate and the
country were those relating to slavery, and growing directly
out of the repeal of the " Missouri Compromise," so called,
prohibiting the establishment of slavery in the Territories
north of 36° 30′ of latitude. The repeal of this provision
by the Kansas-Nebraska Act of 1854, and the subsequent
disorderly and outrageous proceedings in Kansas, for the
purpose of forcing a slave constitution upon her, had profoundly agitated the people of the entire country. Mr.
Foster's first notable speech in the Senate was delivered
on the 25th of June, 1856, during the debate on a bill to

enable the people of Kansas to form a State constitution. This address was marked with calmness and dignity, and yet in its utterances was distinct, manly, and bold. The speaker's hostility to the system of slavery was frankly avowed, while the constitutional rights of the slaveholding States were as frankly conceded. An eloquent vindication was made of the awakening public opinion in the North on the subject of slavery in the Territories, in reply to the sneers at "shrieks for freedom." The participants in the famous public meeting in New Haven to extend aid to the departing emigrants for Kansas were eulogized and defended. The key-note of the speech was sounded in the declaration that the only remedy for the existing excitement was the repeal of that part of the Act organizing the Territory of Kansas which blotted out the Missouri Compromise. The arguments urged by Senator Douglas, the author of the Kansas-Nebraska Bill, in favor of that action, were subjected to sharp analysis, and their inconsistencies exposed in a masterly manner.

This speech established Mr. Foster's position as an able debater in the Senate. It was also received with great favor among observing men in the North, not as an appeal to sectional passion, but as a piece of calm and judicial reasoning, which went direct to the root of the questions at issue. Many letters were received at this time by Mr. Foster from eminent public men, commendatory of the soundness of his positions, and urging him to continue as he had begun.

Two years later, on the 8th and the 19th of March, 1858, the Senate being in committee of the whole upon the bill for the admission of Kansas as a State under the Lecompton Constitution, Mr. Foster again took an emphatic position in respect to the repeal of the Missouri Compromise.

He said, " I believe its repeal was a violation of plighted faith. I believe it was an outrage upon the moral sense of the nation, and it ought not to have been done. I therefore will recognize the old compromise, and will never recognize the repeal." Further on in the debate, in answer to a question from one of the Southern senators, Mr. Foster declared that he would never vote for the admission into the Union of a slave State formed from territory north of the line of the Missouri Compromise. The declaration of one section of the Lecompton Constitution was, that " the right of property is before and higher than any constitutional sanction, and the right of the owner of a slave to such slave and its increase is the same and as inviolable as the right of the owner to any property whatever." This Mr. Foster denounced as " false in morals, false in politics, and false in law ; " and as " a reproach and a shame to the age in which we live." The provision, in the proposed constitution, that no alteration should be made in it to affect the rights of property in the ownership of slaves also received his sharpest criticism and condemnation. On the 8th, in concluding his remarks, — which were made unexpectedly and without preparation, — Mr. Foster said, " I wished to be heard now, even in this very imperfect manner, lest by possibility the vote might be taken here, and my voice never be uplifted against this most atrocious, high-handed act of usurpation." In this debate the rights and duties of Congress in regulating the formation of Territories and the admission of States were thoroughly and logically discussed by Mr. Foster, who bore himself with great calmness and courtesy in the midst of frequent interruptions from Southern senators, on whom the force of his arguments made a palpable impression.

Mr. Foster maintained a firm and consistent position

during all these stormy years which preceded the election of Abraham Lincoln to the presidency. On the 4th of January, 1860, we find him addressing the Senate upon the resolution to print the annual message of President Buchanan. An acrimonious debate had taken place over the references in the message to the absorbing topic of slavery. Mr. Foster's remarks were directed to a recommendation of the President that he be authorized by Congress "to employ a sufficient military force to enter Mexico, for the purpose of obtaining indemnity for the past and security for the future." The condition of the government of Mexico was at that date extremely chaotic; and, amid the contentions of the rival claimants of the presidency, the property and lives of citizens of the United States had been jeopardized. Mr. Foster opposed the recommendation, in a concise and powerful speech, as being unconstitutional, against international law, and as tending to a conquest of Mexico, which was for many reasons undesirable. But the larger portion of his argument was addressed to the inconsistency of an interference with a foreign country for the reasons alleged, while the same abuses and wrongs were perpetrated within our own territory without any effort on the part of our government at redress. He pointedly asked, "Is the life, liberty, or property of an American citizen, within the slaveholding States of this confederacy to-day, who entertains opinions obnoxious to those communities on the subject of slavery, any more safe than the liberty or property of our citizens within the Republic of Mexico?" In illustration of the indignities inflicted in the Southern States upon Northern people suspected of anti-slavery tendencies, he related the experiences of several persons from Connecticut and elsewhere. Among these was that of Mr. James Greenwood, one of Mr. Foster's townsmen, who was driven from Alabama, because his children, while in Norwich, Conn., attended a public school at which a few colored children were present. He referred also to the advertisements in the Southern journals, setting a price upon the heads of Northern abolitionists, to the outrages committed by the polygamists of Utah, and to the bad faith of the government toward certain of the Indian tribes. " I think," he concludes, " it would be much more becoming if the United States in the first place should set the example of good government at home."

In this address, Mr. Foster made a pointed reference to the Southern threats of secession in the event of the election of a Republican President. He avowed his belief that the threats would not be carried out, but urged them as an argument against intrusting President Buchanan with the extraordinary power he desired.

The election of Mr. Lincoln brought matters to a crisis; and Congress assembled in December, 1860, under most serious and agitating circumstances. Five of the Southern States had already begun preparations to secede from the Union, and the entire country was distracted with anxiety and apprehension. On the 10th of December Mr. Powell of Kentucky called up, for action in the Senate, a resolution previously introduced by him for the appointment of a committee of thirteen, to whom should be referred that portion of the President's message referring to " the distracted condition of the country, and the grievances between the slaveholding and the non-slaveholding States." By the terms of the resolution, this committee was to be instructed to inquire whether any legislation " for the protection and security of property in the States and Territories" was needed, and to report upon the expediency of proposing amendments to the Constitution with that end in view. Amendments were at once proposed, to include the rights and security of persons within the committee's sphere of investigation, and to authorize them to inquire whether any further legislation were requisite for the maintenance of the Federal authority. As the debate proceeded, Mr. Powell found it expedient to withdraw all that portion of the resolution which referred to the rights of " property," and limit it to a simple instruction to the committee " to inquire into the present state of the country, and report by bill or otherwise." Upon this proposition an important debate took place, which was watched the country over with intense interest. Jefferson Davis and other secession leaders frankly avowed the opinion that the proposal of a committee was mere political quackery, that legislation and constitutional amendments were valueless, and the only remedy was to be sought in the hearts of the Northern people. Legal guarantees were useless without an entire change of Northern sentiment toward slavery. Indeed, the purpose of the Southern senators was evidently only to secure a more complete acknowledgment of the right of property in slaves as the price of peace. Early in the debate Mr. Foster arose, and briefly expressed his approval of the resolution. He would have voted for it, he said, as originally offered, although he could not commit himself to any suggestions for the amendment of the Constitution, and although he preferred the resolution with the first proposed amendments. As the measure from a member of the party which for years had controlled the administration, and in whose hands the country was said to be falling to pieces, he regarded it as his duty to support it, as one tending to allay the public excitement, and to bring back harmony and fraternal feeling to the country.

At this time Mr. Foster had come to believe that secession and civil war were inevitable. He was among the first who avowed this conviction. On the 1st of January following the debate just referred to, Mr. Foster being absent on a secret mission for the incoming administration, Mrs. Foster represented him at a dinner party given by Mr. Seward. During the conversation she ventured the opinion that the country was drifting into civil war. Senator Preston King of New York laughingly bade her dismiss her fears; when she replied that her husband thought as she did. Thereupon Mr. King turned seriously to her, and inquired if Mr. Foster really entertained such an idea, and, on being assured of the fact, laughed heartily at the absurdity of it. Mr. Seward even more strongly ridiculed such a foreboding. This blindness to the earnest purpose of the Southern leaders was shared by some other sagacious public men. Mr. Foster, however, was oppressed with apprehension, and was prepared to make almost any sacrifice not inconsistent with principle to avert the threatened calamity. His attitude in reference to the proposed committee of thirteen gave rise to considerable criticism among his constituents, and some went so far as to accuse him of "backing down" from his principles. His real sentiments were, however, clearly defined in the following extract from a letter written to a complaining friend, and printed in the public journals:—

"As to yielding the principles for which I, in common with my political associates, have been contending so long, I certainly have not 'backed down,'—do not propose to. Disruption of the Union is, I believe, inevitable. So believing, it does not seem to me desirable to use irritating words, to criminate or recriminate. If disunion be a blessing, we shall be likely to enjoy it. I believe it will lead to war and bloodshed, and I deprecate it. Still, I am opposed to having slavery established or recognized by the Constitution of the country beyond the limits or terms originally assigned to it, be the consequences what they may. To found a government on a principle so clearly violative of human right, so offensive to God, must sooner or later call down His curse. It is surely better that we refuse to incorporate this demand into our organic law, even in view of the most terrible alternative which can be presented. None can be so terrible as the wrath of God, which would surely visit us if we consented to this enormity."

To these convictions Mr. Foster was always loyal. He accepted, however much he regretted it, the fact that slavery was recognized in the Constitution; and he scrupulously respected all the constitutional guarantees, behind which the institution intrenched itself. Yet he profoundly detested the system, and was inflexibly opposed to its further recognition and to its extension over the free territory of the United States. It may be as well here as elsewhere to follow his after course of action on this absorbing public question.

After the outbreak of the rebellion, the slavery problem continued to be no less an embarrassment than before. What disposal to make of the fugitive negroes from the insurrectionary States; how to deprive the slave confederacy of the material aid of the system, and yet act consistently with the rights of slaveholding States which adhered to the Union, were questions involving great perplexity. In the session of 1863 the House of Representatives passed a bill appropriating the sum of ten million dollars to aid the State of Missouri, under certain condi-

tions, in emancipating her slaves. This bill came before
the Senate on the 29th of January, with sundry amendments proposed by the Judiciary Committee, the chief
features of which were the increase of the proposed sum
to twenty million dollars, and the consent to a system of
gradual emancipation, extending over a period limited to
thirteen years. In the discussion which followed, no objection was raised to the principle of compensated emancipation. It had already been applied, in 1862, to the District
of Columbia. The points of difference were respecting
the amounts proposed, and the contemplated extension of
time. Some of the more radical Republican senators
were prepared to vote any amount of money that might be
requisite, but were decidedly opposed to gradual emancipation. Mr. Foster, speaking for the Judiciary Committee
of the Senate, and undoubtedly representing the sentiment
of Mr. Lincoln's administration, advocated the proposed
amendments. The chief consideration urged was, that to
make Missouri a free State would be a fatal blow to the
rebellion. "I believe," he said, "if slavery be abolished
in the State of Missouri, the Southern rebellion will be
more thoroughly crushed than we can do it by armies and
navies." And again, "The State of Missouri I regard
as the ground where the question of this rebellion may
almost with certainty be decided for our country. If we
can make this great State free, millions of money are not
too much." Regarding the concession of gradual emancipation, he said, "I agree that immediate emancipation
would be more coincident with my own feelings ordinarily
than gradual emancipation. . . . Still, if we clearly see that
we cannot abolish slavery in the State at once, shall we
not do it gradually? . . . Shall we peril the great cause

upon this question of emancipation one year from the 1st of January? I should be glad if it could be done; should heartily rejoice at it: but, if it cannot be done in one year, I would rejoice to have it done in thirteen years rather than that it should not be done at all."

The extension of the time of emancipation to thirteen years was permissive, not obligatory; and Mr. Foster and those who thought with him were of opinion that the reform, once begun, would be completed in a far shorter period. It should be said that this bill contemplated payment for all slaves, of rebel or loyal owners, except such as were excluded by the provisions of the Confiscation Act of 1862. Mr. Foster had, at the time of that enactment, favored the manumission by proclamation of all slaves belonging to those who continued in active rebellion for six months after the passage of the bill. However, the scheme for compensated emancipation went to pieces before the great exigencies of the war.

On the 20th of April, 1864, Mr. Foster addressed the Senate on the bill then pending for the repeal of the Fugitive-slave Act of 1850. He was heartily in favor of this bill, believing, as he did, that the Act of 1850 was unconstitutional in its provisions. But an amendment had been offered to save from the operation of the bill the Act of 1793. This amendment was favored by Mr. Foster, in company with Senators Trumbull, Sherman, Collamore, and Harris of his Republican colleagues; and he proceeded with what was intended to be a brief explanation of his vote in its favor. Being interrupted, however, by Mr. Sumner, he was drawn into a somewhat extended debate, in which his objections to the repeal of the Act of 1793 were fully set forth. They may be briefly summarized as follows: the

Act was, in his belief, constitutional, and it had been so declared by the Supreme Court of the United States. Its terms, indeed, were mainly those of the Constitution itself. The Constitution provided for the reclamation of fugitives from labor; and under this provision the owner of the escaped slave was clothed with authority in every State of the Union to seize and recapture his slave. No process of law was necessary. By retaining the law, publicity, delay, and legal restrictions were guaranteed to all such transactions. So far as the States in rebellion were concerned, they were out of the question, inasmuch as their slaves were declared free by the proclamation of President Lincoln on the first day of January, 1863. But there were certain slaveholding States which had kept their faith with the Union, and their constitutional rights should be respected. The law should be permitted to remain upon the statute book until the constitutional amendment abolishing slavery, which had recently been adopted by the Senate with great unanimity, should be ratified, and put an end to slavery forever.

The speech was a purely legal argument, favoring the observance of constitutional forms and obligations, made at a time when the fervor of the public hatred to rebellion and slavery was so intense, that to invoke the Constitution in behalf of the actual rights of partisans of either subjected public men to reproach. During the argument Mr. Foster did not fail to express his life-long hostility to the system of slavery, and his desire for its speedy extinction. Yet his position was widely misunderstood. When, in the course of the debate, Mr. Sumner ventured a reference to Mr. Foster's remarks as "vindicating slavery," he received a reply which silenced him upon this point. But popular misunderstanding was not so easily enlightened. A storm of reproaches, in the newspaper press and in personal correspondence, beat upon the senator's head. He bore it with the greatest serenity, being assured of the soundness of his position and of the rectitude of his motives. He was conscious that his opinions were those of President Lincoln, in whom the people rested the utmost confidence, and those of some of the acutest and most conscientious of his colleagues. He received also many letters expressive of the confidence of the writers, and their admiration of his moral courage under the trying circumstances. Among these was one from the late President Wayland of Brown University, containing this concise expression: "With you, I do not see why Maryland and Delaware, and any loyal slaveholding States, have not the same civil rights as ever. I hope the time has passed for their exercise; but, still, right is right." Undoubtedly this speech created some prejudices which worked to Mr. Foster's disadvantage in Connecticut, when, in 1866, he was a candidate for re-election to the Senate. Yet the great mass of his constituents retained an unshaken confidence in his political integrity, and in his fidelity to his early political faith. It is pleasant, in this connection, to quote from a letter written him in 1866 by one of his constituents, an old-time abolitionist, who, after the utterance of the speech just mentioned, addressed him in most severe and solemn terms of condemnation. He says, —

"In justice to myself as well as to you, I must in all sincerity here say that I have rarely so thoroughly changed my opinion respecting any individual as I have in reference to yourself. . . . I therefore hereby pledge myself to do every thing in my power to continue you in the position you now occupy. If I faithfully keep this promise, I know not what I can do more to prove that I both honor and respect you."

In December, 1866, Mr. Foster spoke and voted against
the bill granting universal suffrage, without distinction of
color, in the District of Columbia, not from any change of
opinion on the subject of slavery, or from any opposition
to the grant of equal rights to colored persons, but because
he favored the qualification of intelligence as it existed in
the State of Connecticut, and which was not required by
the bill. At that period of excitement, however, as the
nation was emerging from its desperate struggle for exist-
ence, a dispassionate consideration of such a question was
impossible. The bill passed both branches of Congress,
and was a second time passed, over the veto of the President; and in the House of Representatives the intelligence
qualification was not even granted the consideration of
debate.

In the course of his remarks on this bill, Mr. Foster
said, "We are not making a law for one year or for two
years, but we are making a law which we ought to consider
perpetual, — a rule for voters, not merely in this district,
but one which ought to be safe and salutary if adopted
throughout the United States." Ten years later, in his last
message to Congress, President Grant directed the attention
of the country to this question. "The compulsory support
of the free schools," he declared, "and the disfranchise-
ment of all who cannot read and write the English language
after a fixed probation, would meet my hearty approval. I
would not make this apply, however, to those already voters,
but I would to all becoming so after the expiration of the
probation fixed upon." At this time public attention was
considerably aroused to the importance of the subject and
to the evils of ignorant suffrage. The foresight of Senator
Foster and the few who stood with him was justified by the

experience of the decade. Nothing practical resulted, however ; and it is not impossible that the golden opportunity for beginning this weighty reform was lost forever by the action of Congress in 1866. A friend writes us, —

"The attitude which Senator Foster assumed upon this subject deserves especial emphasis as being one of the best illustrations of a salient feature of his character. Thousands of sagacious and thoughtful students of our political system, especially those not in official positions, have bemoaned the evils of unrestricted suffrage ; and no intelligent inquirer into the subject to-day can fail to see that the country would be better off for some such discrimination as was contemplated by this bill. But the tide of popular opinion was at the time sweeping toward extreme favor to the liberated slave ; and in standing openly and almost alone by his convictions of what was for the permanent welfare of the nation, in the face of his colleagues' and of his party's criticism, and at the peril of his own official position, Mr. Foster manifested a heroism too unfrequently displayed by those to whose hands the shaping of the public policy of the nation is intrusted."

During the years of the Rebellion, Mr. Foster's services, both in the Senate and out of it, were zealous and patriotic. It has been mentioned that he was among the first to foretell the war. Before its actual outbreak he was prepared to make any concessions, not inconsistent with principle or honor, to avert it. After hostilities began, however, he was untiring in his exertions to promote the triumph of the Union cause. On the 11th of March, 1861, he rose in his seat to move the expulsion of Senator Wigfall of Texas, the latter having declared in debate that he was a foreigner, and owed no allegiance to the government. He supported the resolution by a forcible and pungent speech. The Senate, however, did not choose to take so decided a step, and merely removed the obnoxious senator's name from the rolls.

One of the prominent journals of the day made the following comment upon this occurrence : —

"Of late the inebriated vagabond (Wigfall) has assumed the strutting insolence of the Southern Confederacy, has boldly declared himself out of the Union, and a resident of another nationality, — in short, has as boldly and offensively announced his treason, in season and out of season, as ever did Catiline in the Roman Senate; and we rejoice that, at the least, his impudence and arrogance have been snubbed, if his treason be not visited with the punishment it deserves. We rejoice more than all that it was left for gallant little Connecticut — ever the Thermopylæ of Freedom's battles — to do it, and to do it effectually. Mr. Foster is not a man of hot blood, who acts from sudden impulse. This movement has been one of deliberate judgment, and one in which his sense of duty to his country has triumphed over the timidity which would have deterred most men from administering such a bold, yet richly merited rebuke. For, be it understood, it requires physical as well as moral courage to bring such scoundrels to their reckonings."

Some time later, when a resolution for the expulsion of Senator Bright of Indiana was before the Senate, Mr. Foster incurred some criticism by opposing it as contrary to the former precedent. By this time, however, senators were ready to acknowledge that the former action was a mistake ; and Mr. Foster then withdrew his opposition.

In all measures which came before the Senate having relation to the well-being and efficiency of the army and navy, or calculated to increase the vigor of the struggle against the rebel confederacy, Mr. Foster took an active interest. The bill proposed by him for the care of abandoned cotton lands was highly commended for its practical efficiency. The various confiscation projects received his most careful scrutiny, and his were among the most weighty of the legal arguments made during their consideration. We find him in June, 1862, an ardent advocate of a bill for increasing the medical department of the volunteer service. His remarks in its support revealed an extensive and sympathetic knowledge of the needs and sufferings which existed among the volunteers, owing to the lack of efficiency in the medical organization. In the same session, in considering the appropriation bills, he opposes cutting down the pay of officers of the army or navy. In the next session he opposes the proposal to abolish the military academy at West Point, arguing that the academy was no more responsible for the treason of some of its graduates than Yale or Williams Colleges were for the delinquency of theirs.

In January, 1864, the enrolment bill being under discussion, Mr. Foster exhibited his coolness in opposing an imprudent measure. The North was so exasperated by the cruel treatment of Union prisoners in Virginia, and other parts of the South, that it was seriously proposed in the Senate to authorize the President to call out a hundred thousand volunteers, independently of the draft, to serve for a hundred days, and aid in driving the rebels from Virginia and releasing the prisoners. Mr. Foster in his remarks rendered ample justice to the patriotism of the Northern masses, who would, he said, arouse like the old crusaders at the call of Peter the Hermit. This scheme would, however, divert attention from more permanent and efficient military organization, and he could not feel justified in supporting it. On the 10th of February, 1864, he argued strongly against an amendment to the army bill, increasing the pay of the colored troops, because it was not retroactive in its provisions. Many of the colored soldiers had enlisted, he said, under the promise of their recruiting officers that they should be treated in all respects like the white troops. He was entirely opposed to any discrimination in the pay of the volunteers on account of color. On the 25th of January, 1865, he made a powerful argument against the proposal to retaliate in kind upon rebel prisoners. He recited cases of suffering and death which had come under his own knowledge, — some of them being those of his own townsmen. He advocated such retaliation, shooting and hanging, as was justified by the usages of civilized nations, but protested against an emulation of the barbarities charged upon the rebel officials.

His services outside of the Senate chamber were equally laborious and patriotic. His time and strength were given to every call to patriotic duty. His private correspondence abounds with expressions of his intense and anxious interest. He shared the solicitudes and burdens of President Lincoln, and strengthened him by his counsel and support. He possessed in a high degree Mr. Lincoln's confidence. He was, during one political campaign in Connecticut, subjected to reproaches there for not leaving his post at Washington to take the stump for the Republican candidate. The reproach was entirely unmerited. He remained at the capital at the earnest request of Mr. Lincoln, who considered his services there more valuable to the country than in any other place. Yet we find him at various times addressing large assemblages in Connecticut, rebuking the grumblers, cheering the despondent, and inciting the people to greater sacrifices for the Union.

If he made no parade of patriotism, he nevertheless neglected none of its duties that came within his province. At the time of the first battle of Bull Run, he had driven out to the camp in company with other gentlemen. The conflict having begun, Mr. Foster found a surgeon of one of the Connecticut regiments, who had been placed in charge of a field-hospital, overburdened with wounded men, and without adequate assistance. He promptly volunteered his services, and labored assiduously in the hospital for some hours. At the expiration of that time a charge of the rebel cavalry made the position so perilous, that, at the earnest solicitation of the surgeon, who pointed out his danger as a civilian without military safeguard, he reluctantly relinquished his self-imposed service. He beat a hasty retreat on foot for several miles, and fortunately succeeded in evading the enemy and reaching the Federal lines. His arrival in Washington caused great rejoicing, as a rumor had prevailed that he was among the killed. His miscellaneous personal service at this period was incessant. Correspondents from all parts of the country, very many of them persons utterly unknown to him, besought his influence and aid. Some most pathetic episodes of the war, scarcely known beyond the little circle affected by them, came under his notice through these letters, and elicited his active participation. During the

later years of the war, when Washington was crowded with
wounded soldiers, his services were always at call. Often
he might have been seen late at night, in company with
some anxious visitor, looking up officials in search of
tidings, procuring passes to the front, and, in whatever
way the circumstances demanded, giving time and strength
freely till compelled by sheer exhaustion to retire to rest.

No better illustration of the profound solicitude which
filled Mr. Foster's heart during the anxious years of the
civil war can be given, than his private correspondence
with his wife and other confidential friends. The following
brief extracts are taken from some of these letters: In
July, 1861, after describing the passage of a body of
troops through Washington, he writes, "The waving
banners, the glittering weapons, the thrilling music, the
occasional salute and 'good-by' of a friend, and, above all,
the thought of the sacred cause in which these men were
engaged, affected me deeply. My heart seemed to be
getting up in my throat, and I was several times on the
point of bursting into tears and weeping like a boy." In
May, 1862, he writes, "As I think on the sad condition
of affairs, I feel a sense of oppression almost insupportable.
I know not what is to become of this glorious, so lately
glorious, country. May God help us, for vain would seem
to be the help of man! . . . Just think of the thousands
smitten on the battle-field, whose cries of agony have been
going up for days past, all unheard but by the ear of the
Eternal!"

In July of the same year he writes, "God save the
United States of America, dear, poor, distracted, bleeding
country! These are dark days, and the future shows little
brightness. I know not what is to become of us but; we

must not despair of the Republic." And, a few days later, " Oh ! the poor wounded in hospitals, crowded, sweltering, dying ; and the hundreds, perhaps thousands, lying on the ground in open fields, under this broiling sun, who groan, agonize, bleed, and die. God have mercy upon them ! I am reading Jeremiah in my morning devotions, and have been much struck with some passages I meet : ' Weep ye not for the dead, neither bemoan him ; but weep sore for him that goeth away, for he shall return no more, nor see his native country.' "

In April, 1864, he writes, " All, all depends on Gen. Grant's success. He must succeed, and that soon, or the Republic is lost. Dark is the picture, but we may as well look at it. It is before us, wink as much as we will. I have great hopes, indeed, great confidence ; but time will soon determine." A few days later he says, " My contemplations are of a subdued and rather saddened cast ; but God is merciful, and he will do for us better than our deserts, perhaps better than our plans. Within a few months, perhaps a few weeks, something decisive, I think, must happen. As to our poor and wretched country, —

> ' Our hearts, our hopes, our prayers, our tears,
> Our faith, triumphant o'er our fears,
> Are all with thee, — are all with thee.'

My faith is not always quite triumphant : it does sometimes waver. The ignorance, depravity, and meanness which so often rule the hour are too much for it."

These quotations, exhibiting his mingled anxiety and confidence, and his earnest and constant trust in the divine Disposer of events, might be greatly multiplied ; but these will suffice. Whatever his anxieties, Mr. Foster sought always in public life to manifest a calm and tenacious faith and confidence in the ultimate success of the cause which was so dear to his heart.

One of the journals of his native city, opposed to him in politics, paid the following tribute to his personal devotion : " In the public meetings which were held in this town to provide for raising soldiers for the war, he participated as zealously as any one of our citizens, and contributed as liberally from his purse as any one among us, in proportion to his ability. And, during the extra session of Congress, when they were encamped near Washington, his time and services were always freely at their disposal when they needed any assistance at the departments or elsewhere that he could render them. And we happen to know that his purse was on many occasions open for the aid of the soldiers from this State. When they went to the field, he accompanied them, to aid in hospital duty if his aid were needed, to be near them as a friend, and to do any kindly service for them within his power." It may be truly said that the half of his faithful service in these regards was never publicly known.

On the 29th of January, 1865, at an anniversary meeting of the Christian Commission, held in the House of Representatives at Washington, Mr. Foster delivered a brief address, in which he pointed out some respects in which the war of the Rebellion had been a benefit to the country. " How otherwise," he asked, " could the blessings of freedom have been given to the slave ? How otherwise could the freedom of the press, and the freedom of speech, in the very halls of Congress, have been secured ? How otherwise could the canker of avarice have been eradicated from the heart of the nation, and its great benevolence and liberality have been developed ? "

While earnest and faithful throughout to the cause of the Union, Mr. Foster never cherished bitterness nor malignity toward those whose treason had precipitated the struggle. He was anxious for a restoration of amity and good feeling between the people of the two sections. To this end he was scrupulously in favor of the observance of constitutional forms, and was in sympathy with the reconstruction plans of President Lincoln. This attitude sometimes exposed him to the complaints of the extreme men of his party. Yet, while in his action often independent of the opinion of some of his political friends, he was always consistent, and always inflexible in his patriotism and in his devotion to the cause of freedom and human rights. He did not follow President Johnson in his policy of reconstruction ; and one of his last acts in the Senate was to give his assent, though not entirely unqualified, to the policy of Congress. He did not consider that President Johnson was always as censurable in his political opinions and measures as the general public pronounced him ; and in this judgment impartial history, removed from the prejudice and excitements of the time, is likely to acquiesce.

It is not essential to the purpose of this sketch to trace Mr. Foster's senatorial career minutely in all its details. He was among the senators always one of the busiest, and most punctual to his duties, whether in the committee rooms, or in the public sessions. In the discussion of questions bearing on legal or constitutional points. he was an interested and influential participant. In measures affecting the financial or industrial interests of the country, he was always attentive, and often prominent. His speeches on proposals for taxation were concise and lucid. He was severe in his scrutiny of appropriation bills. " I object" was a not uncommon designation applied to him by the under officials of the Senate, owing to his persistent opposition to the hasty disposal of bills involving questionable appropriations. Without familiarity with the tremendous pressure of work, and the excessive mental and physical fatigue incident to the closing weeks of a parliamentary session, one cannot fully understand and appreciate the conscientious devotion to the public good involved in this conduct. Most of the members are desperate with the accumulation of work, and eager for rest; and, under such circumstances, they are disposed to hurry through important measures, appropriating large sums of money, without heeding sufficiently their defects. One gets a broader, fuller idea of patriotism from such exceptionally patient and conscientious labor, and such courageous disregard of others' personal convenience or good will, for the unrecognized benefit of the country at large. He was an earnest advocate of a protective tariff; and some of his speeches on revenue bills — notably on the 20th of February, 1861, and the 23d of February, 1865 — were powerful arguments in favor of the practical importance of this system to the country. In the latter speech he avowed his belief, that, had it not been for the operation of the protective system, the government would have found itself unable to suppress the rebellion. The bankrupt law, which at the time was a measure of great relief to the distracted business interests of the country, undoubtedly owed its passage by the Senate to Mr. Foster's careful attention to its details, and to his persistent support against great opposition. So thoroughly was he identified with the bill in the Senate, that, although he did not prepare the original draught, it was quite generally referred to in the public press as Mr. Foster's bankrupt bill. It served a useful purpose for several years; and, since its repeal, the demand for some provision to replace it has become pressing. He was also the author of the revised pension law, made necessary by the exigencies of the civil war, and was actively concerned in many other important measures.

As an illustration of the moral and religious attitude maintained by him in the Senate, his remarks on the death of Senator Broderick of California, in 1859, may properly be referred to. That senator was killed in a duel. When the customary resolutions of honor were before the Senate, Mr. Foster arose and opposed them. He referred to the fact that the Federal laws, and the laws of the senator's own State, made duelling a felony. He did not mean to attack the character of the lamented senator, or insult his memory in any manner whatever, aside from the mode in which he met his death; but as he conscientiously believed in and upheld the laws, human and divine, which pronounced duelling criminal, he could not vote for resolutions of honor to the memory of one who had met his death in that manner. "We own," commented a public journal of that day, "that we were surprised that this worthy gentleman was the only man found, in that seemingly dispassionate body, brave enough to utter a sentiment so obviously right and Christian."

Mr. Foster in his public speeches made no display of

religious sentiment, although the force of human obligation to the Divine Being was always presented among his weighty considerations when measures having a moral bearing were under discussion. In his private letters relating to public affairs, however, are to be found abundant and earnest expressions of the sincerest Christian patriotism.

In March, 1865, his influence as presiding officer of the Senate was quietly but effectually exercised in the omission from the committees of two senators whose condition on the floor of the chamber had been at times a reproach to the Senate. If little public mention was made of this conspicuous disapproval of official misconduct, it was none the less observed and commended by leaders of moral sentiment throughout the country.

During the last term of Mr. Foster's senatorial service, he held the position of chairman of the Committee on Pensions. He also occupied the second place on the Committees on Foreign Relations and the Judiciary, thus bearing close relation to some of the most important questions before the Senate. In previous terms he had served on the Committees on Revolutionary Claims, Private Land Claims, Public Lands and Territories.

The greater number of Mr. Foster's intimate senatorial colleagues during this important period have, like himself, passed from earthly service. A few words of reminiscence from some of those who survive him may appropriately be inserted here. Hon. Lyman Trumbull of Illinois, who served with him in the Senate for twelve years, writes as follows: —

"For six years we were both members of the Judiciary Committee, from which emanated much of the most important legislation of Congress during the war. No member of that committee was more useful than Mr. Foster. Always attentive, of quick perception and clear intellect, he did much to mould the legislation of that period. He was a man of conservative views, but had no patience with the men who, in 1860–61, were trying to break up the Union. In his public acts he was governed by his convictions and a high sense of duty. He was no timid patriot, but had the independence and the nerve to go forward when duty called upon him to act. I remember well the sensation produced in the Senate when Mr. Foster, early in 1861, on his own responsibility and without consultation, offered a resolution for the expulsion of Wigfall of Texas, who had declared in his seat that he was a foreigner, and owed no allegiance to the United States. Mr. Foster followed up his resolution with a vigorous and patriotic speech. The Senate, however, at that time, was not prepared for such vigorous and patriotic action. . . . I am sure Connecticut never had a more truthful, upright, and able senator. Of his genial nature, sparkling wit, and bright and sunny private life, it was permitted me to know something. By me he was a friend both loved and honored more than almost any other whose acquaintance I made in public life. I feel that the world is better for his having lived in it, and that I am made poorer by his departure."

Hon. H. B. Anthony of Rhode Island, who also was with Mr. Foster during his entire term, furnishes some recollections, from which is extracted the following : —

"I sat next Mr. Foster in the Senate, and became well acquainted with his ways and manners, always genial, always kind. He was a man of quick perceptions, a prompt and ready debater, a close reasoner, an elegant speaker. He was one of the very best parliamentarians that I ever knew, and an admirable presiding officer, thoroughly versed in parliamentary law and in the rules of the Senate, and ready in the application of them. With all the gravity and dignity of his character, he had a quaint humor that enlivened his discourse, and relieved the tone of serious and stately discussion. When, in the course of a long and wearisome debate, some senator would rise and say, ' I can add nothing to what has already been said on this subject,' Mr. Foster would turn to me, and say, *sotto voce*, ' Well, then, brother, why do you say any thing ? ' Once, when a question was put, Mr. Foster decided ' The ayes have it.' The result was doubted, and some one called for a division. The ayes rose ; and, as they sat down, several of them called out, ' Give it up,' meaning that the decision should stand as first announced. ' But the Chair would like to know which side gives it up,' he said. Mr. Foster commanded the respect of the Senate in an eminent degree, both for his ability and his character, and was held in high esteem by Mr. Lincoln, who often consulted him, and who had high confidence in the soundness of his judgment and the purity of his motives. As a statesman, as a lawyer, and as an orator, Mr. Foster stood in the front rank of his contemporaries. In his death Connecticut loses one of her most eminent citizens, and the country one who has rendered to it high and distinguished service."

On the 6th of March, 1865, Mr. Foster, who had been often called to the chair, and was the favorite presiding officer, was chosen president *pro tem.* of the Senate. Upon the assassination of President Lincoln, some six weeks afterwards, he became acting Vice-President of the United States. This position he held for nearly two years, until the close of his senatorial term. Here he displayed the same conspicuous faithfulness and ability which marked his earlier services as Speaker of the Connecticut House of Representatives, except that years of experience in honorable public service had given him a mellower dignity and a more winning grace. A visitor to the Senate at this period thus describes his appearance, in a published letter : —

"Prominent [in the semicircle of seats around the platform of the Senate] appears the serious face of Mr. Foster. He is undoubtedly one of the ablest presiding officers the Senate has ever possessed. Familiar with parliamentary law, strictly adhering to the forms and customs of the Senate, inflexible in maintaining order and decorum, yet ever kind and courteous, he sits like a stern old judge of ancient times, dispensing justice without fear and without favor."

The added responsibility imposed upon Mr. Foster by this important position was borne by him with great dignity, and yet with no small measure of anxiety. The assassination of President Lincoln had thrown the country into a fever of excitement. The personal demeanor and the declared policy of President Johnson had awakened the keenest apprehensions. In the event of Mr. Johnson's death, the chief magistracy would for the interval devolve upon Mr. Foster ; and at one time he had reason to fear that this unwelcome burden would fall upon him.

A resolution of Congress, approved March 3, 1865, directed the appointment of a special committee " to inquire into the present condition of the Indian tribes, and especially into the manner in which they are treated by the civil and military authorities of the United States." Mr. Foster was appointed one of the members of this committee ; and, as before they set out upon their investigation he had become acting Vice-President of the United States, he was made the prominent figure of the expedition. Attended by a large military escort, the party visited several important points in Colorado and New Mexico, and were received with distinguished honor. At several places the visitors were called upon for addresses. Mr. Foster's remarks on these occasions, which were printed in the local newspapers, exhibited a lively enthusiasm over the magnificence of the West, and an earnest interest in all measures, including the construction of the Pacific Railroad, which conduced to its welfare and progress. Some interesting details of this expedition, from the pen of Hon. James R. Doolittle, who was chairman of the committee, will be found in the appendix.

Mr. Foster entered into this journey with great relish and enthusiasm. The grandeur and beauty of the country filled him with admiration. In one of his letters he says, —

"The Central Park in New York, the finest nobleman's park in England, is not as beautiful as the rolling prairie lying south of Leavenworth. The rounded symmetrical hills, the lines, the curves, all are perfect. Portions bear timber, portions not. Where not, the perfect smoothness of the surface would astonish you. Not a stick or bush or rock or ravine! You could drive a pony carriage over every yard within the circle of vision, and not spill water from the cup of a tulip. You seem to be gazing around in the vernal sunshine upon one broad, bright, unbroken sea of emeralds. The sight is enough to make one wish to break away and run off miscellaneously into space, like a deer or an antelope."

The party set out on the 22d of May from St. Mary's Mission, on the Pottawattomie reservation, Kansas, under escort of Gen. McCook, with a hundred and fifty cavalry and thirty infantry. The infantry, with the visitors, rode in ambulances; but the gentlemen of the committee were also furnished with horses, and Mr. Foster spent much time in the saddle. His letters and diaries contain brief but glowing bits of description of the scenery of the mountain regions. His narrations of incidents on this journey, as was usual with him, were scarcely more than memoranda. His retentive memory made any further record needless. His letters of travel promise "sights of stories" to his friends on his return, — a promise which was always most generously fulfilled.

The party reached Santa Fé, New Mexico, on the 1st of July, and on the 4th a ball was given in their honor. Similar attentions were paid them in other places. At Fort Garland they were met about two miles out by a company of cavalry, which received Mr. Foster with presented arms, and escorted him into the fort under an arch festooned with evergreens, and a flag inscribed "Welcome to Vice-President Lafayette S. Foster." Among the villages of the Pueblos Mr. Foster was received by the Indians and the Mexicans with the utmost respect and veneration. His official dignity made him the greatest "Father" ("Tata") their eyes had ever beheld. Thousands came from all directions to shake hands with him. Some of the descendants of the old Spanish settlers, in their veneration for rank, pressed eagerly forward to kiss his hand. At this time he was the guest of the famous hunter Kit Carson, of whom he wrote, "His nature and manners are gentle and winning as a woman's." After Kit Carson's death, he offered to educate one of his sons.

As the party were leaving Taos, New Mexico, on their return to Denver, they were met by a messenger, bringing to Mr. Foster telegrams from secretaries Seward and Stanton, urging his immediate return to Washington. This was occasioned by apprehensions for the health of President Johnson, who was very ill at the time. On reaching

Denver, Mr. Foster received further telegrams, informing him of Mr. Johnson's restoration, but requesting him not to venture out of reach of the telegraph. During the hurried journey from Taos to Denver, although Mr. Foster found time to appreciate and enjoy the grand and impressive scenery, his mind was deeply burdened with the thought of the grave responsibilities that threatened to rest upon him. It was with intense relief, therefore, that he read the re-assuring telegrams which met him at Denver.

In his opinions upon the Indian question, Mr. Foster was entirely in sympathy with those who took the humane view. He often spoke with feeling of the cruelties which had been practised toward them by the whites, and was sometimes sarcastic in his criticisms of the extravagant financial policy of the Government in dealing with them. " It would be cheaper," he said, " to board every Indian in the country at our first-class hotels, at five dollars a day." He always thought them " more sinned against than sinning."

[Extracts from a letter of Hon. J. R. Doolittle to Mrs. Foster, March 7, 1881.]

. . . "You recollect that Mr. Lincoln's assassination in April, 1865, after our committee was raised, had made Mr. Foster, *de facto*, Vice-President; and therefore, although I, as Chairman of the Senate Committee on Indian Affairs had been selected as Chairman of the Joint Commission to do the work, we all resolved to bring him to the front in all our interviews with the Indians, — not as the Great Father himself, but as the one who stood nearest in that relation, to the dependent Indian tribes. . . .

"Some time in June, the exact date I do not now remember, we set out upon our journey, at the rate of about twenty-five miles a day. The weather was delightful, the air from the mountains, over the plains of Kansas, pure and invigorating. We struck our tents very early in the morning, and made but one march. Without halting we made about twenty-five miles, and then pitched our tents for the night, generally about three or four P.M., near some watering-place. No one could possibly enjoy the horseback rides from about six to eleven o'clock in the morning, before the sun became very hot and oppressive, more than did Mr. Foster. His horse had a very lively and spirited gait ; and he was always at the front, full of humor, enjoying and making others enjoy every thing.

"We had been about two weeks on our journey before any thing of special interest occurred. All at once, about ten o'clock in the morning, an immense herd of buffaloes appeared in sight, about half a mile in front of us. All being mounted, instantly armed themselves with carbines and navy revolvers, and pushed forward at all possible speed, not to throw themselves across the route of the advancing herd, for they would have been overwhelmed — horses and riders — had they done so, but to strike them in their rear and upon their flank.

" Into this wild and dangerous sport Mr. Foster entered with all enthusiasm. An enormous buffalo bull was singled out. He was fired upon, and wounded severely ; but he turned upon his pursuers, whose horses were greatly frightened, and turned back towards our train of teams and soldiers for safety, — the old bull slowly pursuing. As he appeared upon the crest of rising ground, the foremost span of mules caught sight of the gigantic beast. Like a flash of lightning they whirled around and ran at the top of their speed down the sloping prairie for nearly half a mile, upsetting the wagon, and scattering every thing upon the ground. Then followed such a panic among mules, and such cursing and swearing among mule drivers, as none can imagine who never were present on such an occasion. A fortunate shot from a Remington carbine at last brought down the huge and infuriated beast, and peace and tranquillity reigned once more through the whole camp. . . .

" During all this excitement of the chase, and of the panic among the mules of our train, Mr. Foster enjoyed himself immensely. His wit and humor and merry glee were flowing in a continual stream. . . .

"From Maxwell's Ranch, New Mexico, we passed down southwest to Fort Union, where we stopped over for a day or two. Upon resuming our march, passing down on the right side of a valley through which one of the small branches of the Canadian River flows, we had not proceeded many miles when, suddenly, we came to a halt; and the important announcement was made by Gen. McCook, that a whole band of the Mescalèro Apaches had just been captured by a company of our soldiers, and were then *en route* to Fort Union.

"Here was upon the face of things an important event, and one which our committee could not overlook. Gen. McCook, who besides being a good soldier was a very good actor and spoke the Spanish language, determined to introduce the chiefs and warriors of the captive tribe, who understood a little Spanish, to the committee, and especially to the Vice-President of the United States, in becoming style. So every thing was put in the very best order to produce a most profound impression upon the savages. A messenger was sent forward with orders to the officer in command of our victorious troops to bring the captives across the valley to the place where we were halted to receive them.

"The warriors, about forty in number, were on foot. The women with their children, blankets, and other worldly goods were mounted upon ponies. They approached. The tall chief dressed in deer skin, with all his paint and feathers on, came up in grand style and with a certain dignity and grace. He, of course, was the first to be introduced to that high officer who stood second only to the Great Father himself, in the estimation of all the Indian tribes.

"Gen. McCook in his best style and best Spanish made a little speech, and then introduced the head chief of the Mescalèros to the Vice-President. Imagine our astonishment when, instead of taking Mr. Foster's right hand as he extended it to him, the tall chief walked directly up to him in front, and in true Spanish style threw his long arms around and embraced him, — warmly, strongly embraced him, I might say literally 'hugged' him, — ejaculating in Spanish, "Buéno! Buéno!" Then followed the lesser chiefs and warriors one by one, until each had given him the same earnest embrace.

"As the last one left him Mr. Foster breathed deeper and freer, thinking the thing at last was over; but in this he was sadly mistaken, for the real agony was yet to come. Soon as the men had finished, the women began to dismount, and, one after the other, in the same style and with the same words of welcome, gave him the same earnest embraces. As they were not as tall as the men, their painted faces came against the breast and collar of his coat, which, like Joseph's, became a coat of many colors long before the grand ceremony was over.

"When with becoming fortitude and patience he had borne all this grand introduction to an Indian tribe, he quietly suggested that perhaps the other members of the committee would like to go through the same ceremony; which they as quietly declined, asserting that one such ceremony was all-sufficient to establish friendly relations with the captives.

. . . "Having taking considerable testimony at Santa Fé as to the causes which led to the war with the Navajoes, we passed northward up the Rio Grande into the Park, and thence by Fort Garland and the Huerfano Pass over the Rocky Mountains, whose highest peaks were covered with eternal snows, into the valley of the Arkansas. We passed over the mountains on horseback. The scenery was grand and imposing beyond any thing I saw in Switzerland. Of course all this was a source of intense enjoyment to Mr. Foster, awakening in him the deepest enthusiasm. Exhilarated by the sight, a touch of high poetic sentiment would occasionally find *impromptu* expression, or bring out most apt quotations. I wish, for your sake, I could give you his words. But sixteen years have come and gone since we were riding there together; and while his words have faded from my memory, their sweetness and fragrance cling to it still."

In May, 1866, after a close and violent contest, Mr. Foster was defeated in the Republican caucus of the Connecticut Legislature, as a candidate for a third term. It is needless in this place to enter into the details. The opposition was based partly on dissatisfaction with his prudent and conservative policy in the Senate, partly upon ardent personal attachments in other quarters, and partly upon the well-recognized geographical precedents of the State. Undoubtedly at the outset a majority of the Legislature was in his favor. His re-election had been used as a powerful incitement to activity, during the preceding canvass for State officers. It had been accepted by his friends, as an assured fact. Mr. Foster himself, had, as usual, made no exertions to insure his personal triumph. When the sum of a thousand dollars was contributed to the chairman of the Republican State committee, to be exclusively devoted to securing the election to the Legislature of Mr. Foster's friends, he refused to permit the fund to be thus expended, and insisted, that it should be applied to the proper expenses, of the general canvass. But, when the Legislature assembled, powerful influences were brought to bear upon some of the members. Unjustifiable representations were used, with marked consequences. Among these was one, to the effect, that the most eminent of his Republican colleagues in the Senate desired his defeat, on account of his "sympathy" with the policy of Mr. Johnson's administration. This unfounded report brought out denials from several senators. The following, from Senator Fessenden of Maine, at that time the Republican leader of the Senate, was among the number published : —

" I understand that an objection has been made to the re-election of Senator Foster, to the effect that he did not possess the confidence of our friends in the full extent. Upon this point, I feel it my duty to say, that, from the time when Senator Foster took his place in this Senate, I have entertained for him great respect and confidence. I look upon him as one of our most reliable, able, and useful members. I think, that, after the record we have made of twelve years of service in the Senate, it would be unfair to impute to either of us a want of faithfulness to our party obligations, or of devotion to the best interests of the country. There is no ground whatever to doubt the perfect truth and uprightness, in all his relations, of the distinguished senator, who so acceptably presides over the deliberations of the Senate. Be pleased to excuse my thus volunteering to give testimony where I trust none is needed."

Although defeated by a few votes in the nominating caucus, Mr. Foster was urged to stand as an independent candidate, being assured of Democratic support. After deliberation, however, he declined, and peremptorily withdrew his name from before the Legislature, against the remonstrances of prominent Republicans, both at home, and in Washington. To a friend, he wrote, " My withdrawal I regarded as a matter of duty, under all the circumstances : and, that being so, it was certainly a matter of expediency ; for right is the highest expediency." In his defeat, the State of Connecticut exemplified her stubborn adherence to precedent usage, which, at that date, out of twenty senators, who had represented her in Congress, had returned only six for a second term, and for a third term, not one.

Those who knew intimately the value and importance of Mr. Foster's services at Washington, and the influence which he gave to his native State in shaping public policy, were grievously disappointed, at this unlooked-for event. Letters from personal friends, and from men prominent in the public service, poured in from all parts of the country.

One of these, from the pen of Professor Henry, may be properly quoted here as fairly illustrative of the general tone of this correspondence : —

WASHINGTON, SMITHSONIAN INSTITUTION, June 6, 1866.

. . . "I could hardly believe that so enlightened a State as Connecticut, would be so blind to its own honor, and the best interests of the nation, as not to re-elect such a man as Mr. Foster. This thought I shared with every reflecting person who is acquainted with your honored husband, or who has given attention to his public career. It was supposed, that his State would be proud of one, who had so won the confidence and esteem of his companions, as to be unanimously chosen by them, to preside over their deliberations, and to discharge the duties of the second office in the government of the nation.

"I look upon his non-election, as a calamity to the country, both in the loss of his service in the Senate, and in its indication of the spread of the tendency to political changes, which cannot be other than prejudicial, to the best interests of the government. With the increase of our population, and the consequent enlargement of the number of interests involved, the legislation of the nation must every year become more complex and difficult, requiring higher intelligence and greater theoretical, as well as practical, knowledge.

"The business of legislation, like all other pursuits, requires devotion of thought and long experience ; and every year that is added to the term of service of a senator of the character of Mr. Foster, adds to his influence and efficiency. His knowledge of what has been done, and his familiarity with forms, as well as with principles, are of great importance, and must increase in value with the length of service. Fluency of speech and ordinary common sense, even when joined with honesty of purpose, by no means suffice, as qualifications for a proper legislator. Besides these, he must have a mind capable of grasping the widest generalizations, and of logical power, to deduce from them, consequences of immediate applicability to the wants of the time, together with learning, to urge the right in such language, as will command attention and insure conviction, while it is in strict accordance with refined rhetoric, and does credit to the culture, as well as the sagacity, of our legislators.

"When a man of the character of Mr. Foster has been chosen, and has fully developed his powers, he should be kept in the position of a senator, as long as his mental and physical energies will enable him properly to discharge the duties of the office. It was by adopting such a course, that a galaxy of great men were found a few years ago in the Senate of the United States. It was by having ample time allowed them to study the great questions of policy, and to gain the necessary experience in the art of statesmanship, that Webster, Clay, Adams, Benton, and others were enabled to exert so wide and important an influence over the popular mind of the country. If the rule of rotation in office, is to be generally applied to the election of senators, then farewell to the dignity, the wisdom, and integrity of that body, to which we look for the conservative influence and cautious legislation, which alone can perpetuate our present form of government.

"But it is not alone on account of the loss to the nation, that I deeply regret the non-election of Mr. Foster. He is, *ex officio*, one of the regents of this Institution; and I have rejoiced in the expectation of having him a member of the Board of Directors, to whom I could always look with confidence, for counsel and support.

"In this city, I have not spoken with a single person on the subject, who does not regret that Mr. Foster was not re-elected, or who does not consider the fact that he is not, a bad omen for the future of our political condition. But however his non-election may be regretted by others, it can scarcely be considered a source of disquietude to himself, since in political life he must have encountered much at variance with the refined sensibility of his nature; and in the constant pressure of public business he must have longed for the opportunity of calm contemplation so necessary to the cultivation of literature and science, to which his tastes are strongly inclined." . . .

Mr. Foster, however, bore his defeat with characteristic equanimity, and in his after-life found occasions to repay with kindness and aid, some, whose conduct at this time had been unmanly, if not treacherous. His own feelings may be well understood from the following passages of a letter to one of his friends, where his seriousness of character appears in happy contrast with his playful humor : —

"The loss of my election did not seriously affect my digestion or my sleep, and will not, I fancy, affect the crops. . . . The events of one's life do not happen by chance, but are under the control of One who is all-wise and all-merciful. How infinitely little do we know as to what is best for us to-day, much less for to-morrow, next week, or next year! With peace of conscience, and a submissive disposition, we cannot be very far from being happy."

On the 2d of March, 1867, Mr. Foster resigned the office of President of the Senate, his term as a senator being about to expire. Mr. Anthony of Rhode Island, in offering the formal resolution of thanks to the retiring officer, addressed the Senate as follows : —

"Mr. President, I know that I echo the sentiment of every senator upon this floor, to whichever party he may belong, when I bear testimony to the high ability, the uniform courtesy, and the unvarying impartiality, with which the duties of presiding officer have been performed, during the Congress, that is about to close. The chair, sir, to which you have just been called by the unanimous voice of your peers in this chamber, has been filled by election of the Senate, by some of the most eminent men who have embellished the annals of American statesmanship. John Langdon, Richard Henry Lee, Theodore Sedgewick, James Barbour, Nathaniel Macon, William H. Crawford, William R. King, Samuel L. Southard, William P. Maguire, Hugh L. White, Solomon Foot, and others not less eminent, have been president *pro tem.* of the

Senate. It is safe to say, that by none of them, have the duties of the chair been performed, more to the credit of the officer, or more to the satisfaction of the Senate, than by the retiring president, *pro tem.* Fortunate will it be for those who shall succeed him, if, when they come to lay down the high dignity, which he has just resigned, they shall take with them so large a share of the respect, the confidence, and the affection of their associates in this chamber. Fortunate will it be for the Senate, if the same knowledge of parliamentary law, and the same prompt application of its principles, shall guide their discussions, and the same impartial dignity preside over their deliberations."

Mr. Foster's retirement from the Senate, was noticed with very general regret, by the Republican press of the country; although his friend and successor, Gen. O. S. Ferry, fully possessed the confidence of his party. No one was more surprised than Gen. Ferry himself at the result of the senatorial contest; for he was a warm admirer of Mr. Foster, and confidently expected his re-election. Wherever the value of cultivated talents and high personal character in public men was appreciated, the hope was expressed that Mr. Foster would not long remain absent from the councils of the country, where his influence had been so conspicuous and beneficent. One brief notice of his retirement, from one of the daily journals, may be properly quoted here : —

" Almost all of our Republican, and many of our Democratic, exchanges, have referred in most complimentary terms to the late president of the Senate, Hon. L. F. S. Foster. All unite in an indorsement of the tribute paid him by his fellow-senators, as a dignified, courteous, and impartial presiding officer ; and nearly all justly applaud his honorable and useful senatorial career. These expressions of esteem, at this time, must be exceedingly gratifying to the retiring senator, for he has, during his term of office, been sharply criticised at times, by some of those, who are now most cordial in their praise. These criticisms were for the greater part called out by Mr. Foster's alleged conservatism and timidity; yet a review of his record, will show an almost unbroken succession of votes upon the great questions of the day, with which the most exacting radical cannot fail to be satisfied. Naturally prudent, temperate, and cautious, and having a distaste for the rougher and more aggressive methods of carrying out political policy, he has on some occasions, inevitably given offence to those of his party, who, while not more essentially radical than he, have been more sharply stimulated by partisan feeling, or who, with an inflexible determination to push a political principle to the end, have cared less than he, about details, or have had smaller regard for those things which past party traditions had pronounced good, and sufficient. He is not an extremist, and therefore the extreme men of his party have often found him, weighing with caution, opinions adopted by them as correct, beyond question. This we believe to be the extent of what has given rise to criticism of Mr. Foster's career as a statesman. Between him and the great majority of his party, there is an entire sympathy in opinions. At this time, however, criticism is disarmed; for his term of service is ended, and the senator has for the present retired from public duties. Having aided by his eminent and honorable services, in giving Connecticut a fame and influence at the national capital, equal to that, enjoyed by the most illustrious of her sister States, he may be cheered by the reflection, that he occupies in the minds and hearts of those whom he has represented, a position of greater esteem and honor, than at any previous time of his public service."

At the expiration of his senatorial term, in March, 1867, Mr. Foster returned to the practice of the law in Norwich. At this time his name was prominently mentioned in connection with the Austrian mission, then made vacant by the removal of Mr. Motley. It was even alleged by some malicious persons, that he was seeking the office, and that there was doubt of his confirmation by the Senate in the event of his obtaining the appointment. In regard to the latter point, the well-informed " Providence Journal " remarked, " Mr. Foster has been in Washington on strictly professional business. No man in the country is better fitted to serve it at home or abroad ; and, should the President do so sensible and patriotic a thing as to nominate Mr. Foster for any place which he would accept, he would not find it necessary to canvass for a confirmation, among his former associates, whose respect and confidence he possesses, to a degree rarely accorded to any man." Mr. Foster did not receive the nomination. The reason is, no doubt, correctly hinted at in the following statement made at the time by a sagacious newspaper correspondent : " Perhaps at last President Johnson will send in the name of Mr. Foster. The Senate is quite anxious that he shall, and it may be, for that very reason, he refuses to nominate him."

In the spring of 1870 Mr. Foster again represented the town of Norwich in the General Assembly of the State. On being asked if it was not rather a " stepping down " for a man, after having been so long President of the United States Senate, to accept a seat in the State Legislature, he replied, " Not if he is sure he can be useful there. Wherever a man can really do good, there it is no condescension for him to employ himself." He was again elected Speaker of the House, after a unanimous nomination by the Republican caucus. Later in the session, he was chosen associate justice of the Supreme Court of the State, receiving every vote cast in the Senate, and a hundred and ninety-seven, out of two hundred and two, votes in the House. This remarkable unanimity of feeling, on the part of the Legislature, without distinction of party, found expression from Mr. Hamersley of Hartford, one of the prominent Democratic representatives, on the occasion of Mr. Foster's resignation of the Speakership, on the 16th of June. Mr. Hamersley offered the resolution of thanks, and remarked that he knew " it met the views of every member of the House." "This House," he said, " had always, so far as he remembered, had presiding officers who addressed themselves faithfully to the discharge of their duties; but Mr. Foster had never had a superior, as a presiding officer in this House, nor had he a superior, as a presiding officer of that august body, the Senate of the United States. He was glad, that he had been promoted to the highest court in the State with such unanimity, a position which he would fill, with so much credit to himself and service to the State."

In the autumn of this year, after holding his first term of court in June, Judge Foster made a brief trip to Europe. As the time approached for the second term of the court to begin, he was anxious to return to it, being always unwilling, as he expressed it, to " shirk his duties." He therefore left Mrs. Foster in Florence, and hastened northward. Reaching Brussels, he was prostrated by a malarial attack. After a brief delay, however, he was able to proceed as far as London, where he again became ill. There he received the kind attentions of the United States Consul, as in Belgium he had been affectionately attended by his friend Mr. Sanford, the United States Minister to that court. After considerable delay, he took passage on board a steamer bound for Boston, — the only one, by which he could then reach home in season. He had a long and stormy passage. He reached Norwich in the midst of a heavy snow-storm, at nearly midnight of the day before the term of court began. He departed by the first available train for New Haven, and entered the court-room, dinnerless, one of the first of the judges to appear, at the post of service. This energetic and prompt attention to duty, was always characteristic of him.

At the expiration of this term of court, he returned to Europe, and, meeting Mrs. Foster in Geneva, enjoyed a delightful, though hurried trip, of three months through Switzerland and Great Britain. They made a hasty passage through France, the recent termination of the Franco-Prussian War having left that country (Paris especially) in a most disorganized and uninviting condition for travellers. They were among the very first to enter the capital after the Communists had laid down their arms, thinking, that even to see that proud city in ruins, was better than not to see it at all. But it was a painful visit to them, and they hurried across the Channel. In common with hundreds of European tourists at that time, and owing to the especial blunders of a *commissionnaire* to whom, in going over the Alps, they had intrusted them, they lost their trunks, which were not regained until their return to America. In this way a brilliant social career in England, was lost to Mr. Foster; as valuable letters of introduction he had received to eminent personages there, whom he ought to have known, and meant to know, were hopelessly wandering in

those trunks. But this accident gave him the more un-
nterrupted time for sight-seeing, which was diligently
improved.

He held the judgeship till 1876, when, having reached
the age of seventy years, he became disqualified by statu-
tory limitation. During his term upon the bench, Mr.
Foster so bore himself, as to win the esteem and respect of
the bar by his dignity, impartiality, and courteous patience
in attending to the details of cases. In the discharge of
his duties, as superior-court judge, he often manifested the
characteristics of an old-time magistrate, seeking to do
equity, exercising a paternal interest in the affairs of the
litigants before him, and addressing words of kind and
sympathetic counsel, to the unfortunates, whose crimes
brought them under the sentence of the law. The following narration, from the columns of a newspaper of the day,
illustrates one of the finest features in the character of
Judge Foster : —

"Two brothers named Adams, of Westport, had been on un-
friendly terms for several years ; and a short time ago they came to
blows. Each of them complained to a justice, and each of them
was found guilty of a breach of the peace. Both appealed. Their
cases came before the Superior Court last week ; and one of them
was found guilty, and in the case of the other the jury could not
agree. Friday morning, Judge Foster called both of them before
him, and talked to them in a most serious manner, and, after a
short review of the affair, told them that it was entirely wrong and
shameful for them to conduct in such a manner toward each other.
'Even strangers live in peace, and why should not you ? You have
not even the excuse of youth and hot blood, but have arrived at an
age when the passions should be under control.' He then appealed
to one of them, in a slightly sarcastic manner, 'You have always
treated your brother well ?' — 'Yes.' — 'And he has always abused

you?'—'Yes.' He then turned to the other with the same questions, and received similar answers. 'Then,' said he, 'You are both to blame. There is fault on both sides, and I don't know which is the worse.' He then showed them the folly of their present dispute, and admonished them if they had any grievance in the future about property, to either settle it among themselves, or to call in their neighbors to help them. 'But do not go to law: law is an expensive luxury.' Then he appealed to them both to be friends hereafter, and turning to one of them, he put the question solemnly, as in a marriage-service, 'You, —— Adams, do promise on your part that you will be friends in the future with your brother?' The response came ringing out, 'I will.' Then to the other the judge put the same question, 'You, —— Adams, do promise,' etc.; to which came an equally prompt 'I will.'—'Then shake hands,' said the judge; and as they did so there was not a dry eye in the court-room. One of the brothers sobbed out, 'By the blessing of God I will try and live peaceably with my brother.' The other signified the same. 'Then,' said the judge, addressing the one who had been found guilty, 'I impose upon you the lightest sentence of the court, one dollar; and I discharge your bond.' During the closing scenes of this remarkable address of the judge, the State attorney and the members of the bar were all affected to tears."

In this connection it is appropriate to quote the following extracts from a letter written by Mr. H. T. Blake, clerk of the Superior Court of Fairfield County:—

"It is not surprising that Judge Foster stood so high in the affections and honor of the community. Rarely is there united in the same person so much of commanding dignity with so much of gentleness, and even tenderness, of disposition and heart. Many proofs of the latter characteristic might be mentioned. During his official career as judge, it often happened to him to preside in criminal trials; and in these cases especially it was really affecting sometimes to see how beautifully the lofty virtue of the man, as *judge*, mingled with a pity and sorrow and tenderness towards the criminal that was almost womanly. In cases arising out of intemperance, or connected with the sale of intoxicating liquors, his feelings were always particularly warm and deep. I well remember one occasion, when he was delivering his charge to the jury in a criminal case, where one part of the evidence was given by a little boy about twelve years of age, who had been sent by his father on Sunday morning with a tin pail to buy him some rum. When the judge alluded to this testimony, and spoke of the little boy with a tin pail of rum on his way to a drunken father, and meeting other little boys going to church on that bright Sunday morning, his voice faltered; he struggled on; but in spite of himself he became so agitated that he at last broke down entirely, and it was not until after several minutes that he was able to proceed.

"But, while there was so much of gentleness in him, it was not from weakness that it arose. In all matters of duty he was as inflexible as adamant, requiring the strict performance of obligations by others, and, what is much more rare, most rigidly imposing it on himself. I do not know that I could give a better illustration of this than by relating an incident which occurred under my own observation. He was holding court in Bridgeport, and had reached the last court day (Friday, I think) of the week. A case was on trial at noon, very nearly finished; and on coming into court he said (what I never knew him to say before) that he had a very important engagement at Norwich in the evening, and that he was anxious to close the case, if possible, in time to leave on the five o'clock train. All parties assisted in expediting the trial as much as possible; and, as the hour of five approached, the case was substantially finished: lawyers and parties were just preparing to hand in the final papers, and the judge was hastily collecting his memoranda, etc., to depart, when some new idea at the last moment caught the mind of one of the counsel who was noted for his tenacity and tediousness, and he expressed a wish to expand it in an additional argument. 'I will hear you, sir,' said the judge promptly. 'But,' said the lawyer hesitatingly, as he looked at the clock, 'Your Honor wants to leave at five o'clock, and you have now only just time enough to reach the cars.' I looked at the judge's face. It was perfectly grand as he replied without a moment's hesitation, 'That is nothing to the purpose, sir. My duty is here, and my private convenience must give way.' And so he sat unflinchingly to hear a superfluous argument of fifteen minutes in length, and lost the last train for the day, involving a delay of nearly twenty-four hours in reaching Norwich ; nor did I or any one else hear a single expression of impatience or complaint on account of his disappointment or the cause of it.

"I need not refer to his intellectual qualities, his ability displayed in every position of private and public life, his learning as a lawyer, or his spotless personal and political integrity. These were known and read of all men, and have been the themes of numerous eulogies. Nor has it been any part of my purpose to give a general sketch of his character; but I have thought you might be pleased to learn the above incidents, small in themselves, but interesting as thoroughly characteristic of one of whom it can be said with rare fidelity to truth, —

> 'None knew him but to löve him,
> None named him but to praise.'"

Mr. Foster's intellectual qualities appeared to rare advantage during his service upon the Supreme Bench. His strength and readiness of memory were very often exemplified by apt quotations, as the following note, appended to the minutes of the reporter of the court, Mr. John Hooker, in a case argued in Fairfield County, in 1876, will testify : —

"One of the counsel, in his brief, had quoted the well-known passage, 'The discretion of the judge is the law of tyrants,' and ascribed it to Lord Brougham. Judge Foster, at the close of his argument, called his attention to an error he had made as to the author of the remark, stating that it was not Lord Brougham, but Lord Camden, and then went on to give the entire passage, as follows ; — ' The discretion of the judge is the law of tyrants. It is different in different men ; it is casual, and depends upon constitution, temper, and passion. In the best it is oftentimes caprice ; in the worst it is every vice, folly, and passion to which human nature is liable.'

"Judge Foster is most remarkable for his verbal memory. It exceeds that of any one else I have ever known. He is always ready with the happiest of quotations from classical writers and poets, in both English and Latin. He goes off the court next November, when he will have attained the age of seventy. His retirement is a cause of general regret, and to me of absolute sorrow, I have come to feel so great an attachment for him, and to enjoy his society so much."

Mr. Foster's judicial opinions, as recorded in the court registers, exhibit a profound research, and a clear and discriminating judgment. His service as referee, or "committee," as it is legally designated in Connecticut, in a *cause célèbre*, the Nichols divorce suit at Bridgeport, was masterly, and gave him a high and deserved repute. The case was complicated, and the evidence conflicting in the extreme ; but Mr. Foster's findings were universally acquiesced in as conclusive and just.

In the case of Goodwin *vs.* the New York, New Haven, and Hartford Railroad Company, he condemns the custom of giving free passes to public officers, and especially judges, and enforces the necessity of purity in the administration of justice. He says, —

"The administration of justice should not only be pure, but, as far as possible, free from suspicion. That a gift perverteth the ways of judgment, is a truth coming to us with so lofty a sanction that it may not be questioned. Lord Chief Justice Hale, whom Lord Campbell justly describes an object of admiration and love to all his cotemporaries, and as a model of public and private virtue to succeeding generations, refused to try the cause of a party who had sent him a present of some venison, until his butler had ascertained and paid its full value. The payment being refused, the cause was postponed. This by some was thought to be over-scrupulous, and possibly it may have been so ; but, for myself, I prefer on this subject to err with Lord Hale rather than to follow Lord Bacon."

In the case of Kirtland *vs.* Hotchkiss (Conn. Reports 42, p. 442), a suit to recover taxes assessed upon a' sum of money loaned in Chicago, and secured by a mortgage upon real estate there, Mr. Foster delivered an elaborate opinion, dissenting from the other judges. This opinion has been described as, "in point of legal and economic wisdom, and clearness of reasoning, confessedly equal to any similar opinion that has heretofore emanated from the Connecticut bench." The point of the opinion is expressed in this statement : "Property and a debt (considered as a representative of the property pledged for its payment) constitute together but one subject for the purpose of taxation. . . . The debt, indeed, aside from the property behind it, and of which it is the representative, is simply worthless." The *situs* of the debt in question being in Illinois, Mr. Foster held that it ought not to be taxed in Connecticut. As the majority of the court sustained the Connecticut practice of taxing money loaned on foreign mortgage, this case was appealed to the Supreme Court of the United States. There the decision of the Connecticut court was sustained, though mainly on the ground that it was a matter for a State to regulate at its discretion, and not one that the Supreme Court could review. The philosophy of the matter, into which Judge Foster's opinion entered so deeply, was not discussed at any length by the higher court. This and some others of Judge Foster's opinions are worthy of more extended consideration than falls within the scope of this brief memorial. An exhaustive review, with citations, of the Kirtland opinion, was contributed by Hon. David A. Wells to the columns of the " Atlantic Monthly " for September, 1877.

In February, 1875, while yet serving upon the bench, Mr. Foster was nominated for representative in Congress by " a convention of delegates representing the Democrats and liberal Republicans, and all other electors of the third congressional district who do not approve of the usurpations and corruptions of the present administration of the Federal government." This nomination was in opposition to Mr. Foster's wishes, and was accepted by him with great reluctance, in the belief that it was his duty. Mr. Foster had earnestly advocated the election of Gen. Grant in 1868, but, like many other eminent Republicans, had become dissatisfied with the policy of his administration, and believed the tendencies of an influential portion of the Republican leadership were toward corruption. He had in 1872 given his support to Horace Greeley for the presidency, although he did not prefer him as a candidate to represent his opinions. On the occasion of his nomination to Congress, Mr. Foster received the trust " not as a party man in the partisan sense of the term," as he declared in his formal letter of acquiescence. His opinions respecting the existing state of public affairs were not presented in any detail in this document, but are given in a more elaborate manuscript, which he prepared at the time, but was persuaded not to make public. From this paper it appears that he was extremely dissatisfied with the financial policy of the Government. He characterized it as vague and contradictory, and calculated to continue the depression of the business interests of the country. He declared himself emphatically in favor of hard money and a sound currency. He also expressed great dissatisfaction with the Southern policy of the administration, avowing his belief that the army should be entirely withdrawn, or at least not kept in the South as a menace. He referred to the disasters brought to the South by the "carpet-bag" governments, and expressed his belief that the only remedy was to intrust the government to the hands of the native citizens. He did not apprehend any war of races, or any continued oppression of the blacks. The blacks he declared to be no wards of the Government, entitled to special protection, but citizens like the whites, and entitled to the same and no more privileges. He would leave contested election questions to the constitutional tribunals, and not decide them by the bayonet. If these tribunals settled them unjustly, he would still prefer such decisions to right ones compelled by military force. He would only resort to the strong arm of the Government in the constitutional way, in the case of disorders beyond the power of the local government to quell. He would entirely abandon the coercive policy. "If," he says, "we cannot win back the South by words and deeds of kindness and friendship, they will not be won. We shall never win them by force. No people are ever worth winning in that way." Mr. Foster did not, either in this document or in his public acceptance, avow any conviction that the Democratic party would, if successful, adopt any wiser policy, but he thought any change would be an improvement. "What I look for," he says in this unpublished manuscript, "and pray for most of all is, that, a change being effected, the best men, the wisest men of all parties, will unite cordially together, and establish a policy which shall, with the divine blessing, give peace and happiness, prosperity and perpetuity, to these United States of America."

Mr. Foster received very little support in the congressional canvass from the Republicans of the third district, which was always strongly radical. He took his defeat, which he anticipated, calmly and cheerfully, sustained by the consciousness that he had endeavored to do right. He was spared long enough to see his opinions on the subject of the Southern policy shared by President Grant, and carried out by President Hayes, whose nomination he warmly approved, presiding over a public meeting held in Norwich to ratify it. He also had the satisfaction of seeing the Republican administrative policy tend in the direction of financial soundness and honesty. The nomination of Gen. Garfield, in 1880, for the presidential succession, gave him great pleasure. This congressional canvass was Mr. Foster's last participation in an elective political contest. In 1877 he was again nominated by the Republicans of Norwich to represent the town in the General Assembly, but declined the honor, owing to business and personal engagements.

On the 24th of May, 1876, with reference to Mr. Foster's retirement from the bench, " The Norwich Bulletin " said, —

" Mention was made yesterday, in our report of the proceedings of the General Assembly, that the governor had laid before that body a letter from Judge Foster, resigning his place upon the Supreme Court bench of the State, in accordance with that provision of the Constitution which limits the service of judges by the attainment of the age of seventy. Although this resignation will not take effect until the second Monday of next November, yet its presentation was necessary at this time in order that the General Assembly, now in session, might fill the coming vacancy. Indeed, it has been anticipated for weeks ; and already the respective merits of the candidates for the succession have been publicly and widely canvassed.

"Mr. Foster's withdrawal from the judicial service of the State is a subject for profound regret, inasmuch as he yet maintains his full intellectual and bodily vigor, with a promise of doing so for many years to come, and has performed the duties of his office with an application to labor, conscientious purity of motive, and a degree of ability which we regret are so seldom equalled. Both nature and experience have combined to qualify him for service on the bench. He possesses a dignity of spirit, a deep, instinctive sense of justice, a keenness of perception, and a broad comprehensiveness of view, richly developed by his long experience at the bar, his service in the state and national councils, and his presidencies of the Connecticut House of Representatives and the United States Senate.

" This penetration and love of right was ever noticeable in his charges to juries in criminal cases, when he exposes the true merits of the case, and clears away the fine-spun cobwebs of the argument in a manner appalling to both prisoner and counsel. Indeed, lawyers who have occasion to advocate divorces, with a poor case and an *ex parte* hearing, have learned by experience to evade, if possible, the risk of his sharp cross-examination of witnesses, intended to get at the truth they are striving to conceal. And yet, while vigorous and even stern in his search for, and maintenance of, the right, he possesses a singularly humane disposition, manifested in his frequent and generally successful efforts to reconcile the contending parties in litigation, and in the tenderness and discretion of his remarks to culprits, especially the young, in imposing sentences.

"The promptness of his rulings reveals great quickness of intellect, in which respect he is particularly well fitted for Superior Court duty. However, he tends away from, rather than toward, technicalities. This trait, his horror of verbosity, and the breadth of view which enables one to see clearly all the salient points above the multiplicity of minor details, give character to his opinions, when serving in the Supreme Court. Another quality, for the observance of which the Superior Court affords better play than the Supreme, is that marked dignity with which he presides, which is almost austere, yet ever graceful ; which unbends at times to a happy bit of facetiousness, yet firmly restrains levity, discountenances artifice and slip-shod work, and commands the respect and even the awe of the bar. This seems to spring from the man's estimation of the spirit above the law, and his own profound reverence of the eternal source of all law. Thus justice and its administration become clothed with a majesty and sacredness too great to allow of wrangling, trickery, or shallowness, and worthy only of the serious and most earnest endeavors of its profound advocates.

"It has not been our aim to tell the full worth of Mr. Foster as a Judge. To do so now might not be within the limits of propriety, even were it within our power. But we cannot let the occasion of his resignation pass without some faint tribute to the eminent ability that has characterized this branch of his service to the State, and the expression of deep regret that it is so near its end."

After his retirement from the bench, Judge Foster resumed the practice of the law in Norwich, and continued in it, during his remaining years. His services were eagerly sought for in intricate and important cases, and his later efforts as an advocate, were among the ablest and most brilliant of his life. It was the universal testimony of his legal associates, that never had he exhibited more strikingly that keen analysis of causes, which always distinguished him as a lawyer, and never did he appeal with more commanding influence, to the jury. On many occasions his services were given gratuitously to necessitous clients, whose claims appealed to his sense of justice. One of these causes, at least, in which he won a brilliant victory over a formidable array of counsel, will not soon be lost from the reminiscences of the New London County bar. From the first to the last of his legal career he was an enthusiastic lover of his profession. At the time of his second election to the Senate, in 1860, he writes to a friend, " I am glad to be re-elected. As I was a candidate, it would have been unpleasant to be beaten. . . . The position is a pleasant one, certainly, quite the most so of any in our government. Yet, for myself, I confess I prize professional honors — those of my own profession — more than any political distinction. Professional honors are not won without deserving them. Political preferment may be gained without merit, and lost without crime."

In July, 1869, Mr. Foster had been tendered an election to the Kent Professorship of Law in Yale College. After holding it under advisement for some months, as solicited, he declined it, mainly on account of his attachments to Norwich, as a home and place of residence. After his retirement from the supreme bench, however, he became a special lecturer in the law school of the university, on "Parliamentary Law and Methods of Legislation." His first course of lectures was delivered in November, 1877, and the last in June, 1880. On the occasion of the anniversary exercises of the school, on the 25th of June, 1879, he gave a most instructive and valuable address on "The Legal Profession the Great Advocate and Supporter of Human Freedom." In this address he thus effectively treated one of the most perplexing ethical questions connected with the practice of law.

"The course pursued by advocates in defending individuals charged with crime has been severely put to question. Cases are by no means rare in practice where a man's professional duty seems to come in conflict with his duty as a citizen. This conflict can be but a seeming one, for surely duties never clash. A man by becoming a lawyer is not absolved from the due performance of all, nor of any, of the duties which are devolved upon him as a man and a citizen. These are of paramount obligation; and if he cannot discharge the obligation and be a lawyer, he must cease to be a lawyer.

"Take a case of every-day occurrence. A man is brought before a court, and charged with crime. He is asked if he wishes for counsel, and he replies that he does. Our law charitably and properly supposes him innocent till the contrary appears, and counsel is assigned him. He then confers with his counsel, asserts his entire innocence, wishes to enter his plea of not guilty, and take his trial.

"Now, suppose the advocate, knowing nothing whatever of the man or of the real facts of the case but what is gathered from the appearance and manner of the man himself, forms an unfavorable opinion: he strongly suspects, perhaps believes, the man to be guilty, in spite of his protestations to the contrary. Shall the advocate therefore refuse to aid him in his defence?

"The most rigid moralist would, I think, hardly justify such a course ; for the result manifestly would be, that the accused, if tried at all, must be tried without counsel, and that because his counsel had become satisfied of his guilt. In all doubtful cases, that circumstance would be conclusive, and conviction would be inevitable ; and the mischief of all this would be, that a man would be convicted, not by the judgment of his peers and the law of the land, but by the mere suspicion, or by the belief, without a word of proper evidence, of the lawyer assigned to defend him. The great wrong of this need not be argued. It is not assuming more than must be readily granted, that, in such a case the advocate should go on and defend the man whose defence had been assigned to him.

"The trial then proceeds. The witnesses come forward and give their testimony. One link after another in the chain, which always connects the crime with the criminal, is supplied ; and the advocate feels satisfied that the accused is guilty. What is now his duty ? Shall he abandon the cause, and leave the accused to his fate ?

"No, he must not ; nor does he violate any duty which he, as a man, owes to society in continuing to aid in the defence of an individual after satisfactory evidence of criminality has been adduced against him. But do you not thus make it the business of a lawyer to screen the guilty from punishment ? By no means. However guilty a man may be, he is still entitled to a full and fair trial, under the law ; and a trial can be neither full nor fair if counsel, at any stage, when personally satisfied of the guilt of the accused, may throw up the defence.

"There is among many people a clear misconception of the theory of an advocate's duty in criminal trials. It seems to be supposed, that, if engaged for the accused, he must, if he can, get him clear, guilty or not guilty. There can be no more egregious error. It is the province and duty of the advocate to interpose all legal defences for the benefit and protection of his client, and to see to it that no grounds·are taken against him, but such as are warranted by law. This being done, whether the accused be acquitted or convicted, the duty of the advocate is done.

"Suppose that while a trial is in progress the accused admits his guilt to his counsel, but still insists on having the trial proceed, and on having a defence made, what shall the counsel do? The situation is most painful, certainly, especially if the life of the accused be involved. The trial of Courvoissier, who was convicted of the murder of Lord William Russell, not many years ago, in England, was an instance of this kind. The trial had been in progress several days, the prisoner asserting his innocence, when he suddenly took his counsel aside, and told them that he was guilty. Mr. Charles Phillips, one of his counsel, then said to him that he doubtless wished to change his plea, and plead guilty; but he replied, no, and insisted that the trial should go on, and that every ground of defence should be pressed to the utmost. The subsequent conduct of Mr. Phillips in the argument of the cause was very severely criticised at the time, and was afterward very fully discussed in the law periodicals. So far as Mr. Phillips endeavored to criminate others, or to excite suspicions against others, whom he knew to be innocent, though his design was merely to save his client's life, his course was more than unjustifiable, it was criminal; and he would deserve the severest condemnation. So far as he endeavored to secure to his client a fair trial merely, he was to be justified; for to do that he had not only a right, but it was his duty."

His interest was warmly enlisted in the prosperity of the school, and in his last will and testament he left an ample provision for the ultimate endowment of a professorship of English common law. His connection with educational interests was not limited to the law school. Though absorbed by the cares and occupations of public life, he always found time and thought to devote to institutions of learning. He was a trustee of the Norwich Free Academy, of which he was one of the original founders, and to which he bequeathed his fine residence and grounds in Norwich, subject to the life tenure of his widow. He also bequeathed funds for the foundation of a scholarship at Brown University.

During his later life, Mr. Foster, aside from his professional occupation, was actively engaged in many matters of public interest. During the years 1878 and 1879 he served with honor as a member of the commission, on the part of Connecticut, to settle the disputed boundary question between that State and New York. Subsequently, this disagreement being adjusted, he was appointed by Gov. Andrews one of three commissioners to negotiate with the State of New York for the purchase of Fisher's Island. He was also one of the commissioners appointed in 1878 to inquire in the feasibility of simplifying the system of legal procedure ; and the rules and forms adopted by them were approved by the judges, and have become the practice of the Connecticut courts. He was a member of the International Code Conference of America, — a volunteer association, co-operating with similar associations of eminent jurists in other countries, — and was a participant in its efforts to promote the codification of the laws of nations, in order to substitute for war a peaceful method of settling international disputes. He was an interested member, and one of the officers, of the Social Science Association. He was the president of the New London County Historical Society from the time of its organization until his death ; was a constant attendant of its meetings, and took a deep interest in all that pertained to its operations. He was an honorary member of the Cobden Club of London ; and although he never publicly abandoned his well known opinion of the necessity of the protective tariff system to American prosperity, he in his later years inclined to believe that the period of this necessity was passing away.

He bore an important part in many of the religious activities of the day, and was a valued counsellor in some of the chief religious organizations. He was one of the vice-presidents of the Congregational Union, and of the American Bible Society. It was announced in the religious press, after his death, that, but for that sad event, he was about to be elected to the presidency of the last-named society. In 1879 he was appointed a delegate of the evangelical alliance of the United States to the general conference of that body at Basle, Switzerland. His services as presiding officer at religious conventions were eagerly sought; and his addresses on such occasions were marked by simple practicality, and an earnest sympathy in the well-being of his fellow-men. He was president of the Connecticut Congregational Club, an organization formed in 1877 for the purpose of promoting acquaintance and co-operation for Christian purposes between the Congregationalists, lay and ministerial, of the State. He was appointed in 1879 a member of a committee which was constituted by the Congregational General Association of Connecticut, for the purpose of seeking a reform in the statutes of the State relating to divorce. The committee consisted of three clergymen and two laymen. It held a meeting for organization; and to Mr. Foster, with Mr. Baldwin of New Haven, was committed the subject of " Divorce Proceedings." Soon after this Mr. Foster went South, and did not meet again with the committee. The loss of his valuable aid was deeply regretted. His opinions in opposition to the laxity of the existing laws and practice were well known. As a judge he was noted for his uprightness and justice in divorce cases, where his influence was wholesome, and where he was thoroughly feared by unscrupulous attorneys.

During the years between 1870 and 1880 his name was often before the public in connection with the filling of important vacancies in the public service, the last prominent suggestion having relation to the vacant English mission in 1879, for which his knowledge of international law and diplomatic usage, added to his eminent intellectual and social qualities, made him peculiarly fitted. None of these suggestions, however, were of his own prompting. Though never guilty of avoiding a public responsibility, he never sought one; and his last years were passed in a serene contentment with the inconspicuous duties of private life.

His last appearance on a public occasion was at the ninety-ninth anniversary of the battle of Groton Heights, opposite New London. Here, on the 6th of September, 1880, on the site of old Fort Griswold, he delivered the last of a long series of public addresses, — an oration burning with that intense love of his native land which characterized him from the days when he sat upon his father's knee, listening to the old Revolutionary tales.

The closing years of Mr. Foster's long and useful life were mostly spent in his beautiful home at Norwich. During the winter months indeed, for the enjoyment of a milder climate and a larger social life, it was his wont (with Mrs. Foster) to go South, staying some weeks usually, *en route*, in New York. His last winter was partly passed in

Bermuda, and, had he lived a few months longer, he was designing to visit California. His physical and mental vigor continued unimpaired. To all outward appearance he was a younger and fresher man at seventy-three, than most of his contemporaries at sixty. His home being a mile from the business centre of the city, it was his habit, in all weathers, to walk back and forth, often several times a day. His studious habits were maintained, his interest in all public affairs was unabated, his zeal in keeping abreast of the current of thought and opinion in the scientific, literary, and other fields of research was unquenched; his flow of spirits and genial wit, still undiminished, made him more than ever the charm of the refined social circle.

The passing years had only mellowed his character, and softened that stern dignity which, by one unacquainted with him, might sometimes have been mistaken for austerity. His life-record had borne the test of contemporary judgment; old political hostilities were forgotten; the purity of his aims and the integrity of his conduct had disarmed all enmities on the part of those with whom his life was brought in contact. His active form passed up and down the streets of his native city, followed by the honoring glances of his towns-people, and by the benedictions and prayers of many humble souls. Few might so fitly be pointed out to the young as the exemplar of what was worthy of their emulation, as this Connecticut statesman in his declining years.

Suddenly he was called to depart. On Sunday, the 12th of September, 1880, he was present at church as usual, and attended to his customary religious duties. On Monday he was taken ill with a light malarial fever, which gave his wife and physician little anxiety until Friday afternoon, when a congestive chill suddenly seized him, which was the work of Death. He became instantly delirious, and afterward relapsed into unconsciousness from which he never rallied, but, on the succeeding Sunday morning, the 19th of September, 1880, he painlessly and peacefully passed away.

Mr. Foster's character and abilities were conspicuously revealed during his long course of public service, yet his finer qualities were in a measure hidden except to those who knew him intimately. His aims in life were lofty and pure, and, while he was ambitious of success, he scorned to seek it by unworthy means. At the time of his first visit to Washington, shortly after his admission to the bar, he was ascending the steps of the Capitol when the thought came to him, "Shall I ever occupy a seat within these walls?" His ambition was fired by the suggestion; and he said to himself that he would at least strive to qualify himself for a position in the Senate, and, if he did not succeed in gaining it, he would hope to have merited it. This incident he related later in life to a friend who congratulated him upon his first election as United States Senator. Though in his earlier life active in politics, he was never a politician, in the professional sense of the term. He was indeed sometimes almost too negligent of the more ordinary and trivial methods of gaining popular favor. He

was a believer in political parties, and was scrupulous
about party usages. His training as a lawyer and parliamentarian made him deferential to precedents. He was,
however, more independent of party opinion than of party
usage. He often drew upon himself the criticisms of
members of his party for his conscientious differences from
the popular sentiment. Yet he used to remark that his
record in votes, and in fidelity to party traditions and
practices, was far more perfect than that of some of his
colleagues to whom his critics were wont to point as
examples. He was characteristically cautious in his action
upon public measures, especially those of doubtful utility,
or involving an untried policy. This caution, combined
with his courteous deference to the opinions and interests
of others, was sometimes mistaken for timidity. Those
who knew him well did not require a vindication from this
charge; while for those who did not, there is in the long
record of his public speeches and acts, a sufficient evidence
of his steadfast moral courage.

He was a ready debater and an acute logician. He
relished the excitement of reasonable debate, most keenly.
The following extract from a letter written by him after the
close of an exciting trial, at the time when he was coming
into prominence as a member of the bar, well illustrates
his fondness for forensic contests: "How exhausting," he
writes, "and yet how thrilling, how ennobling, is a fierce
intellectual struggle with generous antagonists! Nothing
so certainly and so speedily wrinkles the brow, and showers
the snow-flakes upon the head, — nothing so drinks up
what Madame de Staël so felicitously calls 'the sap of
life,' — as violent mental effort. And yet I love it. Dearly
do I love the excitement produced by the collision of intel-

lect with intellect. The onset, the strife, the doubt, the hope, the triumph of victory, — I love them all as well as Julius Cæsar loved war." His speeches in the Senate were often far from ornate ; yet his remarks on measures in which he was deeply interested, and to which he had given much thought, abound in eloquent passages. He was apt at quotation ; but, except the citation of authorities in support of an argument, he rarely used the gift in debate. His speeches were calm and dispassionate, and were often models of logical arrangement and analysis. His discriminations were nice. A favorite form of attack was to place his antagonist in the predicament which, as he reasoned, he would be brought into by his own argument, and then make the absurdity of it apparent, — a form of the *reductio ad absurdum.*

His keen sense of humor sometimes found expression in irony, uttered with such profound gravity as to completely deceive the listener. A good illustration of it is found in his speech on the Lecompton Constitution, delivered in the Senate on the 8th of March, 1858. Mr. Foster quoted from the proposed constitution the phrase " Free negroes shall not be permitted to live in the State under any circumstances," and proceeded with the utmost seriousness to comment upon the barbarity of a constitutional provision for offering free negroes in sacrifice. There was no power in the Constitution, he argued, to put them out of the State ; the laws of adjacent States prohibited their entrance therein ; by the proposed constitution of Kansas they could not " live " within her boundaries, — therefore nothing was left but to kill them. Some of the opposing senators fell into the trap, and seriously and elaborately denied that any state constitution authorized free negroes to be put to death.

His candor in giving the arguments of his opponents full force, won him the universal respect of his colleagues. On one occasion, in debate in the Senate, an eminent antagonist on the Democratic side paid him the marked compliment of saying, " I know there is no person within these walls, who, I think, would be more frank in the statement of the position occupied by one with whom he does not agree, than the Senator from Connecticut."

Mr. Foster's speeches were always the utterance of profound and earnest conviction. They came from a warm, tender heart, as well as from the head ; which fact imparted wonderful dignity and fascination to his delivery. These were enhanced by his almost entire freedom from manuscript or notes. So carefully matured was his thought, so clear his mental vision, and so strong his grasp of a subject, that no interruptions, however artful or sudden, could ruffle his temper, or divert him from his main argument, although he sometimes indulged in repartee, the swiftness and keenness of which exposed his interlocutor to utter ridicule, and made him feared by his best equipped antagonists in the Senate.

His intimacy with President Lincoln made him to a certain extent a spokesman for the administration. On this account his remarks on important measures of public policy were received with deference ; and his thorough information in respect to matters of fact in possession of the executive often threw light upon important questions before the Senate.

On points of parliamentary precedent or senatorial usage, his utterances, even when not occupying the chair, were usually deferred to, as authoritative. His memory on such points was wonderfully tenacious, as evinced on one or two occasions, when senators who disputed him thought they spoke from the record. His manner was dignified, deliberate, emphatic, and persuasive. He was always listened to by his colleagues with marked attention and respect; for his speeches were practical, and addressed rather to the judgment of the Senate than to the emotions of the people.

Mr. Foster despised trickery and pretence, and was not always careful to avoid offending those who practised them. Persons who sought his aid in attaining mere selfish or personal ends were often received with coldness, if not repulsed. Moreover, it sometimes appeared as if some of his early diffidence clung to him through all his years of public life. This was especially manifest in his dealings with those who only knew him slightly. Constituents who sought his assistance at Washington sometimes felt, after an interview, that they had made no definite progress with him in furthering their affairs. On the other hand, Mr. Foster found himself embarrassed to know precisely what they desired of him. An explanatory word from some mutual friend quickly cleared up the obscurity; and the visitor would depart from Washington with the conviction that the reserved senator was, after all, a most whole-souled and helpful man. He did not, indeed, readily reveal to strangers that personal magnetism which so endeared him to his chosen friends. He was slow to manifest the familiarity of confidence, but, when that was attained, he could not do too much for those who shared it.

Other people estimated Mr. Foster's talents more highly than he did himself. He was free from conceit. He had not a spark of vanity. While he never pretended to be what he was not, he often made no pretence of being what he really was. He was, in fact, a man of rare mental power, and of extensive literary acquirement. His whole life was one of assiduous study. His love of science was marked. Professor Henry said of him, that, were he not so accomplished and useful as a statesman, he should feel that he had mistaken his vocation, in not devoting himself to scientific researches. He was profoundly versed in history, for which he had a passion. He was familiar with the choicest morsels of English and classical literature. There was, however, no display of erudition in his public addresses, or in his ordinary conversation. The revealing of his literary treasures, was reserved for more intimate occasions. His recitations of long and beautiful passages, both in prose and poetry, with which his wonderful memory was stored, will always remain among his friends' most charming recollections of him. While spicy and witty in conversation and debate, quick to detect and to assail the vulnerable points in his opponents' arguments, he was often reticent of his own opinions, and not forward in defending them. Nor was he over prompt to vindicate his motives, preferring often to suffer the sting of misrepresentation, rather than parade his sacred convictions.

The purity of his public life, and the integrity of his character, were never impeached or questioned. Political foes, united with political friends, in giving testimony to his worth in these respects. If he ever betrayed a marked asperity of demeanor, it was in collision with men whose aims and motives were corrupt or low. Ordinary self-seeking he met with coldness; but base and mercenary policy he looked upon with contempt.

In his social life, he was a rare companion. His flow of genial and witty conversation, made him a favorite in the most cultivated circles. His refined tastes, his chivalrous

regard for woman, his stores of literary lore, his acute
observation of persons and things, furnished to the guests
in his own hospitable home, or to those who elsewhere
enjoyed his intimacy, an intellectual feast not often excelled. The following glowing, but well deserved, tribute
to Mr. Foster's personal and social qualities, is from the
pen of one whose knowledge and appreciation of cultivated
society qualify her to testify : —

"It seems impossible, in the memory of that modesty which
never was at fault, to say all that one would like to say of Judge
Foster. It seems almost as if that small delicate hand would be
raised in deprecation, that the old familiar gleeful laugh would
come, and that some bright speech would drop from his lips to
turn our compliment to jest. ' *We cannot make him dead !*'

"Judge Foster had no pretension, he was too great for that;
he almost erred on the other side, and disliked compliment. If he
ever referred to himself, it was to make gentle fun of those who,
feeling how superior he was, would sometimes fain flatter him.

" He belonged to those days when men aspired to be agreeable,
well read, good talkers, and wits. And nature had made him a
wit. He and the Hon. George T. Davis of Greenfield used to
divide New England between them, as the sayers of good things,
Mr. Foster's wit being, perhaps, the keener of the two.

" He had not only *wit* but *humor.* His heart overflowed with
tenderness and pity and love; and George Eliot's exquisite defini-
tion of humor, ' to feel sad, but to talk gayly about it,' was a
perfect description of his delightfully tender humor. At times Mr.
Foster's conversation was poetical ; it was lofty, refined, learned,
always varied and instructive. He had all the strange mixture of
smartness, thrift, prudence, excellent common sense, keen satire,
and perfect insight into character, which belongs to the true New
Englander, but he had also a Grecian, a classic elegance in his
intellect. He loved the beautiful in every thing. There was
nothing in music, sculpture, painting, or nature too fine for his

high recognition. His was a rounded nature. He was a full-grown, gifted man, with every faculty at its best development. If the word 'delightful' had never been invented, it would have been coined to express Mr. Foster. His cordiality, his beaming and ready greeting, his love for his friends, his perfect sympathy, his determination to be agreeable under any circumstances, the wit which flowed from his lips perpetually, as a fountain springs into the air, — all, all, as healthful, as cleanly, and as pure as the fountain, the waters of which sweeten the air, and catch a thousand rainbows from the sun; his remarkable powers of conversation, seizing the inspiration of the moment, tossing back the ball of talk full of repartee; excellent at a quotation; and above and beyond all this, a charm which cannot be described, so wholly his own, that the people who loved him best and knew him best feel inadequate to express him, — such was our lost friend. This fine-tempered man, during his long life at Washington, so full of honor as it was, was the idol of society. No man, perhaps, was so sought for as a social inspiration.

"'To put Mr. Foster between two dull people makes them both gay,' said a lady who greatly admired him. It was difficult to believe, in seeing Mr. Foster, so shy and shrinking was he of any pretence, that this was the dignified statesman, the Vice-President, the lawyer of name and fame, and the much-courted and witty personage of society. He seemed rather to be hanging on the lips of the person speaking to him, and he put every one at his ease.

"He liked society, and would go to a dinner and two or three parties of an evening, if a lady desired to take him! And what an attendant was he on such occasions! The truest gentleman, respecting and admiring and reverencing women; so full of tact, so full of grace, so humble, yet so gay, so good, and so witty, and so much amused; these were golden opportunities of meeting a man, of whom the grand old name of 'gentleman' was the fittingest title!

"Mr. Foster may be counted as among those who had tasted of all life's best blessings, and but few of its griefs and sorrows. And

how he gave out love, sympathy, and friendship, those whom he
honored with his friendship only know. He had more friends than
any other man, almost ; and he deserved them. Not only honor but
love, not only love but confidence, not only confidence but intense
respect, these were the feelings inspired by him whom we shall
always mourn, the Hon. Lafayette S. Foster."

M. E. W. S.

Though naturally grave and serious in aspect, his enjoyment of a hearty laugh was something unique, and
magnetic in its effects upon those who beheld it. His
merriment seemed to begin inwardly, first revealing itself
by droll twitchings of the mouth and twinklings of the
eyes, and ending by convulsive shakings which were
speedily shared by all present. His humor was quaint,
and his wit often caustic ; but his frolicsome moods were
almost infantile in their freshness and abandon. His
genuine appreciation of fun betrayed itself not only in the
trivial matters of daily life, but often on more formal and
decorous occasions. The dry debates of the Senate were
frequently enlivened by his quip and repartee.

The recollection of Mr. Foster's wit and humor, both
serious and merry, is still fresh in the minds of all his
friends. Yet it would be vain to attempt to record these
flashes, which sprang from the suggestions of the moment.
The fine flavor of sparkling conversation, or of repartee,
like the bouquet of old wine, vanishes with the occasions
enlivened by them. Not only was he a good talker, but a
good listener as well, and had the happy faculty of putting
those he conversed with on good terms with themselves.

These genial qualities of the departed senator were but
one form of expression of that exquisite sensibility of
character, which was manifested also in the tenderness

of his affections. His was a sensitive nature. He was uncommonly acute in his social sensibilities. He was so prostrated by the death of his last child that a trip to Europe was found necessary to rouse him, by change of scene, from his profound depression. During his whole life he observed the birthdays of his three little ones who died in their early childhood. Some of his letters, written even in his latest years, contain most touching allusions to these bereavements.

Among the tributes to his memory which were published after Mr. Foster's death was the following, from one of his associates at the bar, which exemplifies the tenderness of his social nature : —

"EDITOR OF THE BULLETIN, — Will you please allow me a few words of respect and love to the memory of the late Lafayette S. Foster ?

"Much has been said of him as a learned judge, an illustrious statesman, and an eloquent advocate ; but I desire to relate an incident, if such it may be called, showing the man in the tender and social relations of life, and in which he seemed almost to forecast the near future when he should go hence, recalling so tenderly sad memories of the past.

"I had occasion, in the month of October last, to correspond with him. In the closing paragraph of one of his letters he said, 'Your sun is high in the meridian, while mine is far in the west. Happily, no dark clouds border the horizon.' The letter was so beautiful, that, upon reading it to my wife, she said, 'Keep that letter to read by and by to the little boys.' I wrote to Mr. Foster that we should carefully preserve his letter for the purpose named, and soon received this reply, with the lines of poetry : —

"'I did not suppose that there was any thing in my last letter to you that would be of any interest to Mrs. ——. She seems, however, to have the invaluable faculty of extracting something good out of every thing, for the benefit of her dear boys, — hers and yours. She manifestly feels toward them as Cornelia, the mother of the Gracchi, felt toward hers. The companion lady asked to see her jewels, having first shown her own. Cornelia showed her sons.

"'These dear boys of yours will, I hope, prove jewels in a higher and better than any earthly sense. Once I, too, had objects of the fondest and tenderest affection, — three loved and darling ones. It is just thirty-eight years ago this very day since my first-born — a bright, beautiful boy, none more so ever gladdened a parent's heart — faded away, at the close of his second summer. His two sisters, no less attractive, the oldest less than four years old, now lie side by side with him on the banks of the Yantic, almost in sight of my windows.

> " ' " But, by faith, I see the shining
> Of the crowns of peace entwining
> Spirit-brows, all white and pearly,
> Of the loved who left us early,
> Seeking rest." '

"Doubtless what he saw by faith has ended in the fruition of victory, and ere this he has imprinted a father's kiss upon those 'darling ones' who left him early, 'seeking rest.'

"The last time I met him was a few days before receiving the letter, when, in company with another friend, we spent a good part of a pleasant afternoon in a drive to Roseland Park, and over the beautiful hills of Woodstock. He was very happy that afternoon. I shall never forget the charm of his conversation, so full of instruction, good sense, good humor, and sparkling with wit. And, as he repeated the whole of 'Alnwick Castle,' by Fitz-Greene Halleck, I listened with a pleasure never to be forgotten. My friend and I have recalled the occasion many times since.

> " ' He was a scholar, and a ripe and good one ;
> Exceeding wise, fair-spoken, and persuading ;
> Lofty, sometimes sour, to them that loved him not ;
> But, to those who sought and loved him, sweet as summer.'

" Death has unloosed his royal spirit from the captivity of earth,
and has opened to it the gate of a higher and nobler fame than any
he enjoyed on earth."

G. W. PHILLIPS.

At the time when he was urged to accept the Kent Professorship at the Yale Law School, which would involve a
removal to New Haven, Mr. Foster remarked, " How could
I ever leave the graves of those children, and their mother?
If it were the desert of Sahara, I would never pitch my tent
elsewhere. It would kill me, to tear up my roots here."
Yet he never intruded his sorrows upon his friends, but
bore them, ordinarily, in silence, and with Christian fortitude. Few strangers who beheld his grave and impassive
demeanor would suspect, what a depth of exquisite tenderness was hidden beneath it. This temperament displayed
itself in thoughtful kindnesses to others, which were always as unobtrusive as they were delicate. But it is not
needful to dwell upon his many kind and gentle deeds.
Wherever he lived, the memory of them is written upon
thankful hearts.

" When the eye saw him, it blessed him ; and when the
ear heard him, it took knowledge of him."

A few extracts from a chapter of simple reminiscences,
written by one of Mr. Foster's life-long friends, may appropriately find a place here : —

. . . " Let me name one trait that tended to make him so great
a favorite in home and social life, and that was his never intruding
the perplexities and burdens of professional and public life among
those who could neither share nor relieve them. In the long and
close acquaintance of many years I cannot recall a single instance
in which his business cares were intruded upon his friends. . . .

"To all who knew him, even casually, his quick repartee and humorous perception of things was most apparent. And yet his wit, though pointed, was never bitter. His gift in conversation was unchallenged, yet he was as truthful as he was humorous. He was playfully accused one day that in telling a story he had '*stretched it.*' 'I did it on purpose, my dear friend. I never mean that a story shall pass through my hands like clipped coin. I always mean to give a little better than I receive,' he returned with a merry laugh, that told the point. Being invited to take tea with a family of relatives, with his wife, she went early and alone, with apologies for Mr. Foster's absence. With her constant thoughtfulness she feared the table would be too crowded. Just as the social meal had commenced, Mr. Foster's welcome arrival was announced. Mrs. Foster, looking up, with a tone of mild reproach, said, 'My dear, I told you not to come till after tea.' — 'And that is just what I *have* come after,' was the response, as amid the applause of all a seat was found for him in the circle of which he was the life and delight. And his repartees seemed so natural one wondered they had not occurred to himself. One cold, raw day some one said 'The wind was searching.' — 'I would not mind its being *searching*, if it was not *finding*,' he replied with a shiver.

"Speaking one day to a friend in Hartford of the eccentric behavior of a common acquaintance, it was said, 'We should call such a one deranged here, and put him in the Retreat.' — 'Oh! *we* have no such institution, and cannot afford to have our standard of sanity so high as you have in Hartford,' he quickly replied.

. . . "How shall I speak of the times when the lives of his little children filled his heart with the tenderest affection, even when every hour was crowded with business cares? Three beautiful children were born to him, but each little life closed before another took its place; so that three times the parents were left childless. After the darling little Joanna and the noble boy, Alfred Standish, had lived to be loved and pass away, little Mary came to fill the sad vacancy. One present in church at the baptism of this beautiful child said it was almost painful to see how intently the father watched the darling, drawing the wrappings about the little form, dreading lest any breath of summer air should visit her too roughly. Not long before she was taken from them a friend took a pencil likeness of the lovely infant, which was the only memorial of her beauty when she had passed away. The bereaved mother loved to recall in this the features of her child, but it caused Mr. Foster such convulsions of grief he could not look upon it. Yet this mourning was not unsubmissive, but tender and affectionate. He found the lonely mother one day so overwhelmed with sorrow, that, after speaking words of comfort in vain, he said, in tones she could never forget, 'I should think you had lost your God.' This implied reproach came home to her with great force, and stilled all thought of murmuring."

S. D. H.

The crowning grace of Mr. Foster's character was his profound, yet childlike, Christian faith. It illumined his inner life, tempered and sweetened his self-respect, inspired his courses of action, entered into his convictions upon public questions, prompted his secret and open charities, and breathed through his prayers and religious teachings. He became a member of the First Congregational Church of Norwich Town in 1832, and in 1836 united by letter with the Second Congregational Church at Norwich. He was a constant attendant at church, and, after the first few months of his membership, participated actively in its social meetings. His political interests and pursuits never seemed to quench his religious fervor. In 1872, at the formation of the Park Church in Norwich, he transferred his connection thither, and, to the day of his death, was one of its most steadfast and devoted members. He also conducted a large Bible class in the Sunday school. In one of the letters received after his death the following reference occurs to this faithful labor : —

. . . "The death of Judge Foster has prompted me to offer my humble tribute of respect to his memory. If he is deserving of honor for his ability as a statesman, and for his incorruptibility as a judge, he is entitled to still greater respect for his fidelity in Christian duty. For nearly four years it was my privilege to be the superintendent of the Sunday school with which Judge Foster was connected as teacher of the Bible class. No teacher in the school was more punctual in attendance, or more conscientious in the performance of every duty. Ever ready to devote his talents to the various departments of Christian work, it was in the Sunday school that he exhibited his rare qualities of mind and heart to the best advantage. It was here that the simplicity of his Christian faith, the extent of his Biblical knowledge, and his broad Christian culture, were most conspicuous. The simple presence of such a man in the Sunday school was an inspiration to all associated with him. Honorable as was his position when presiding officer of the United States Senate, he was even more honored as a faithful Sunday school teacher. The work that he performed in this capacity will endure long after the other has passed from the memory of men. God hasten the day when more men like Lafayette S. Foster shall attain to their highest dignity by teaching God's Word in the Sunday schools of our land!" . . .

G. W. H.

No sketch of Mr. Foster's life would be complete which did not touch upon the depth and sincerity of his religious character. By nature he was possessed of a quick and fiery temper. One of his friends, to whom a similar temperament, but uncontrolled, had proved a bane to his life, once asked Mr. Foster if he supposed he could ever overcome and rule his spirit. His reply was, "Certainly. I had a far more hasty and impetuous spirit than yourself in my youth, and even up to the time of my beginning the practice of the law. In my first case at court, I lost my temper, appeared to disadvantage in the eyes of others, and wounded my self-respect. I said to myself then, that if I was to succeed in my profession, that temper must be controlled; and I made that conquest the first business of my life." In wonderful contrast to this tempestuous beginning were all the subsequent years of his life. He was remarkable for the meekness of his bearing, his unruffled composure under provocation, and his patience and sweetness in adversity. This beautiful self-discipline, which was the grand underlying secret of his quiet strength; the unspotted integrity of his public and private life; his broad humanity, sympathizing ever with the wants and sorrows of his fellow-men; his solicitous interest in the welfare of all religious and philanthropic enterprises, all bear witness to the Christian faith and Christian principle that guided him. These evidences of faith give confidence to those who mourn him, that, when the unexpected summons called him from a ripe and vigorous mortality to cross the threshold of the unseen and eternal world, his soul was found in readiness.

After his death, the book-mark of the pocket Testament which had been his familiar companion was found placed over these words : " For we know that if our earthly house of this tabernacle were dissolved, we have a building of God, a house not made with hands, eternal in the heavens."

From a Marble Bust executed by C. Calverley,
New York, 1879.

APPENDIX.

I.

THE LATE SENATOR FOSTER.

OBSEQUIES OF THE FALLEN STATESMAN. — GREAT CONCOURSE OF FRIENDS. — IMPRESSIVE SERVICES. — ELOQUENT ADDRESS BY DR. BACON.

[From "The Norwich Bulletin" of Sept. 24, 1880.]

THE mortal remains of the late Senator Foster were consigned to the grave in Yantic Cemetery yesterday afternoon, after a prayer at his late residence in the presence of a few intimate friends, and public services at Park Congregational church. The latter were attended by a large concourse of people, many of them from out of town, and holding prominent social and official positions, beside relatives and connections of the family.

The church was full to its utmost capacity, and the most prominent families of the city were represented in the throng. * * *

* * * The service consisted of two fervent and touching prayers, the reading of singularly apt selections from the Psalms in an impressive manner, an address of about ten minutes' length by the pastor, the Rev. Dr. Bacon, and some exquisitely rendered music by a quartet from the church choir. The latter included an anthem by Lyle, made up of verses from the 103d and 13th Psalms, beginning, " Like as a father pitieth his children," and Schubert's " Rock of Ages." As the congregation dispersed, Mr. Kies played Chopin's funeral march on the organ. The whole was in perfect keeping with the profound solemnity of the occasion. Dr. Bacon's

address, which we give herewith, was delivered with dignity and deep feeling, and produced a sensible impression.

"God hath spoken once; twice have I heard this; that power belongeth unto God. Also unto thee, O Lord, belongeth mercy.'

"God hath spoken once, twice; and we have heard his speech, and are afraid. He hath spoken in his holy Word, telling us how frail we are, bidding us to number our days, and apply our hearts unto wisdom; and we have paid little heed. And now, by the mouth of his solemn providence, he hath spoken a second time, with sharp and sudden utterance; and we cannot refuse to hear, and we cannot mistake his meaning.

" He has spoken to the strong man in the splendid vigor of his mature and venerable age; and his word is this, 'To God belongeth power.' He has summoned away the wise man, whose perspicacious mind, enriched with the study and experience of threescore years and ten, was beginning to

'attain
To something of prophetic strain;'

and his lesson to our hearts is this: 'To God belongeth wisdom.' From the dwindling roll of those great statesmen whose public virtue, whose persistent hope that would never despair of the Republic, whose sagacious mind penetrating darkness and disentangling complexities, held the great places of the nation, and guided the country through her awful crisis while all the world looked on — has been stricken off another, and not the least illustrious name; and the word that the event speaks to us is this, that God alone is great. We miss henceforth from our streets, our congregations of worship, our charitable councils, our studies for the good of men and for the glory of God our Saviour, a righteous man, a living example of uprightness, a living rebuke to the base elements in public life, a childlike believer, a humble worshipper of God, called away from us to judgment and to the sweet realization of the divine forgiveness, in the promise of which he trusted. And the departure of such an one to be judged and to be forgiven, speaks to us of the sole, bright example of One who needeth no forgiveness; and bids us lift up our hearts and sing, —

' For Thou only art holy.
Thou only art the Lord.
Thou only, O Christ! with the Holy Ghost,
Art most high in the glory of God the Father;'

and the lesson which it teaches us is this, that 'with him is forgiveness, that he may be feared, and with him is plenteous redemption.'

"And since God is speaking to us so plainly, our words may well be few. Thanks to the dear example of Him who wept beside the grave of Lazarus, it is not forbidden us at such a time to mourn while we give thanks, — to speak with tears of the good gift which we have lost, while we give praise to Him, the Giver, and say our farewell in Christian hope.

"Farewell, great citizen, incorruptible senator, wise counsellor, eloquent advocate, righteous judge !

"Farewell, O faithful friend ! We give thanks at the remembrance of the words of counsel, the acts of kindness, the secret gifts of charity, which he thought were hidden, but the secret of which begins now to be unlocked by his death.

"Farewell, dear fellow-disciple of the blessed Lord, fellow-worshipper with us in His house, fellow-guest with us at His table, fellow-laborer with us in His kingdom ! We give thee God-speed from thy labor to thy rest, from thy waiting and hoping to thy large reward, from these dim visions in which we see as through a glass darkly to where thou seest face to face, and knowest as thou art known. Farewell !

"And he *shall* fare well. To our parting words there comes back an echo from the word of God : 'Say ye to the righteous that it shall be well with him.' We who follow him wherein he followed Christ shall not be divided from him, but with him shall be 'ever with the Lord.' Comfort thyself, O desolate and widowed heart ! O brethren, friends, bereaved together in this great loss, comfort one another with these words !"

The bell, which so often had summoned Mr. Foster to public prayer, tolled as he came to and went from the church for the last time. A long train of carriages, and hundreds of those who afoot paid the homage of following the dead to its final resting-place, proceeded to the cemetery; and it was noticeable that this company of loyal friends included the poor and humble, as well as the rich and distinguished. Perhaps the former had better occasion to mourn. A brief recognition of the supremacy of divine power, and a committal of dust to dust, was followed by the singing of two verses of that beautiful hymn "Abide with Me," in a most affecting manner. After a benediction, the scattering of flowers by loving hands into the tomb, and a lingering farewell, the dead was left to the autumn sunlight and the falling leaves, to the memories and love of those who knew him, and the peace of ever-lasting rest.

Flags on Franklin Square, the city hall, the shipping, and else-where in the city yesterday were at half-mast, out of respect to the memory of Senator Foster.

II.

LAFAYETTE S. FOSTER.

[From "The Norwich Star" of Sept. 20, 1880.]

THE news of the death of Lafayette S. Foster of this city falls upon the members of this community with almost the shock of a personal bereavement. Upon the members of this community, do we say? Nay. The sorrow and profound regret that must accom-pany the mournful intelligence cannot be restricted by the narrow limits of a little township, neither boundaries of county, nor the yet wider lines of state. The removal of such a man — a leader in the vanguard of the intellectual, the Christian, enlightenment of his age — is no small affliction. It is a loss to the nation and to the world.

It is an old truth — as old as the world, and reiterated in every passing moment — that the coming of death is always sudden and unexpected. But a few days ago Mr. Foster was apparently in the possession of his wonted health and strength. He was occupied with the performance of the duties of the present and with plans for the future. Notwithstanding he had passed that stage in life that is generally accepted as the end of the journey, his form was still unshaken, his activity undecreased, and his mental powers, far from being dimmed, seemed to be growing brighter in the glowing ripeness of the perfect autumn. It seemed so unnatural that a life that yet promised so abundantly, should be rudely smitten; and so unforeseen had been the event, that, when the first vague rumor passed through the town, it was received with an emotion of painful incredulity that has not yet entirely vanished.

It is not our intention to attempt a review of the life of this man whose death we now mourn and deplore. His public life is familiar to us all; for its history is inwoven with the history of his town, his state, and of the nation. Words, however tenderly inspired, are but vain and incompetent agents to bear tribute to grand and worthy deeds. Yet there is one lesson that was patiently wrought in the life of the man who is now dead, that it is the duty of every worker for the general weal to present, as well as he is able, to the earnest consideration of society. The lesson is this: That the life that has just closed illustrates, in a remarkable degree, how much grander and nobler is the character that is the outgrowth of substantial and durable talents, united with an incorruptible spirit, than the ephemeral brightness of superficial accomplishments, — tawdry veneering that catches and holds the popular fancy until the polish is tarnished, or its shallowness is exposed. Mr. Foster served his generation and his age efficiently, worthily. And, when he laid down the instruments of his labor forever, his hands were unsoiled by a dishonorable act. No one who knew and appreciated his great mental endowments, his sagacity, and the indomitable resolution of his character, can doubt that his light might have shown more ostentatiously, though with less pure, less lofty and lasting flame, had he consented to sell his birthright for a mess of pottage, to degrade his manhood and corrupt his soul with the filthy attachments of partisan fealty. Intrenched in the integrity of his principles and animated by pure and sincere motives, he acted according to his convictions in every emergency of life. He obeyed the dictates of his conscience rather than the dictates of party or policy; preferring the steady and superior position conferred by fixed principles, rather than the dazzling but evanescent success of a selfish and pliable purpose. Because he did this, the lesson of his life is of inestimable value to all men, and especially to those whose life is yet before them. Because he did this, all men whose admiration is worth gaining shall bend in respectful, grateful homage to his memory. The lesson of such a life, like the fragrance of some rare perfumes, does not die away in a day, but lingers long after the body that gave it expression has disappeared, growing even sweeter and more potent with the lapse of years. The life that teaches such a lesson is worth living.

III.

A TRIBUTE.

[From "The Norwich Bulletin" of Sept. 24, 1880.]

ONE who knew and revered Judge Foster sends us this communication : —

"Mr. EDITOR, — In asking the privilege of your columns to supplement what has been said of the late Lafayette S. Foster, I am conscious that it is impossible to pay him any thing like a just tribute. The virtues of such a noble life were too many, too rare, too subtle to be fully discerned by one person, or, indeed, to be discerned at all, except by the eye of sympathy ; and even then they were to be felt rather than to be described. Mr. Foster was many times animated with purposes too lofty to be understood by the great majority of other people ; and yet, though exquisitely sensitive to ignorant or malicious criticism, he seldom deigned to explanation or self-defence. Rather than degrade a worthy cause by adapting it to gross understandings, or withdraw the veil of modesty from a consciously and exceptionally worthy intent, he would silently endure the torture of misinterpretation or abuse. Such calm fortitude, for truth, for conviction, was almost divine. Yet exhilarated with the purer atmosphere of the mountain tops, he often forgot his comparative isolation, and dreamed not how far away he was from his fellow mortals in the plains below ; nor could they catch an inkling of what he saw and felt on those heights of instinct and will.

"Assiduous and varied industry was one of the most striking traits of Mr. Foster's character. This is best illustrated, perhaps, by the fact that without outside help he rose from the station of an humble country lad to eminence as a lawyer, judge, orator, and statesman. But even richer fruit of his toil was found in the breadth of his culture, the wonderful stores of knowledge which he accumulated, and his persistent devotion, even when he no longer held office, and had reached the ripe age of threescore years and ten, to personal business, public affairs, and intellectual and social pursuits. No mere greed of gain, nor a wish for empty fame, impelled him to excellence in his profession, but zeal to know what other states and nations than his own had done in the science of government. Hence his profound interest in the movement for an international code, and his passion for ancient and modern, personal and political history. Refined and eager taste of course gave direction to this restless activity. He revelled in the choicest literature of his mother tongue, committing numberless passages of rare beauty, and often of great length, to memory. He kept close track of the discoveries of modern science, and the exploits of great men, the world over. And while natural gifts accounted in a great measure for the sparkle of his conversation, the wittiness of his anecdotes, the courtliness of his manners, the grace and pathos of his oratory, there can be no doubt that patient self-training added to the power and charm of his influence.

" Mr. Foster had great breadth of mental vision. He was of a judicial cast of mind naturally. He never took partial and narrow views of things. This was true, not only of his admirable service on the bench, but of his career as a senator and as an individual; and without doubt this trait had much to do with the reliance which Abraham Lincoln — noble, temperate, humane Lincoln — placed on him as a counsellor amid the perplexities and awful responsibilities of the war. Mr. Foster could not be partisan; neither could Mr. Lincoln. Mr. Foster resisted with great effect the spread of slavery as a cruelty and a denial of human rights; in the days of reconstruction his separation from the more radical elements of the party was due to a fear that the North might be cruel and unjust to the whites of the South. He feared lest the re-action from wrong in one direction be followed by wrong in the opposite. When he felt dissatisfaction with governmental abuses in Grant's administration, he only found fault with what had disgraced previous democratic *régimes.* He was consistent. He abated nothing of his devotion to the rights of man meantime, only he was not narrow minded. If, as regards the tariff question, he inclined to the views of Richard Cobden, it was because he included in his scope not merely one nation, but all nations of the world. Yet this breadth of view and this liberality of spirit never left him indecisive and vacillating, as it does men of less concentration of intellect and less energy; but he was strong in his convictions, clear though resolute, and fearless amid criticism. Not merely in politics, but in religion, business, literary and social matters, he had a reason for the faith that was in him.

"Mr. Foster's sagacity foresaw the war before most of his senatorial *confrères,* and he would have gone farther than some of them to avert that calamity; but when that war was precipitated treasonably, he was for prosecuting the defence of the Union with unrelenting vigor. Mr. Foster's secret and public service between 1855 and 1867 contributed much to the abolition of slavery and the preservation of the Union. His public usefulness did not stop here. Like Carl Schurz and George William Curtis, he has contributed much to the purification of civil government in this country.

"What was of infinitely greater value than any other characteristic of Mr. Foster, was the depth of Christian principle which sprang from his religious faith, and pervaded his whole life. It underlay his gentlemanly bearing; it shone through his hospitality; it inspired the generosity with which he spoke and thought of other men; it dictated a thousand acts of secret but bounteous benevolence of which the world never knew; it found expression in the assistance which he gave to religious enterprises; it ennobled his conceptions of the duties of his profession; it imparted a royal dignity and singular righteousness to his judicial decisions; it gave fire to his oratory; it was the key to his patriotism and the mainspring of his statesmanship; it fired his hate of insincerity; it intensified his scorn for the trickery and truckling of mean men. It did not merely adorn a useful life; it gave potency to his whole career.

"Such hard-working, large-minded, high-souled men are important factors in our civilization; they leave permanent impress upon the character of those about them, and upon the civic and other institutions of the country; and they stimulate others to nobler and more efficient lives. So that while those who knew him and loved him will feel keenly the loss of companionship and helpful inspiration, and while faithful adherents of every cause with which he was identified will mourn the cessation of his direct assistance, the age may well thank God that Lafayette S. Foster was spared to so rich a fruitage of actual service, and that his influence will not cease until the ripples of finite time break soft on eternity's shore."

J. H.

IV.

THE LATE LAFAYETTE S. FOSTER.

TESTIMONY OF THE BAR OF NEW LONDON COUNTY.

At the session of the Superior Court, held at New London, in and for New London County, Tuesday, Sept. 28, 1880, Hon. John D. Park, Chief Justice, presiding, the following action was taken concerning the death of Judge Foster.

At noon the Hon. Augustus Brandegee rose, and remarked that the hour had arrived when, by previous agreement, the bar of New London County were to take action appropriate to the death of Judge Foster, and listen to a eulogy prepared by the chairman of the association. Col. John T. Wait thereupon said, —

"May it please your Honor, — At a meeting of the bar of New London County, held on the twenty-second day of the present month, at the court room in the city of Norwich, a committee was appointed to draft resolutions that would embody the sentiments of the members of the bar upon the removal by death of their distinguished brother, — the Hon. Lafayette S. Foster. These resolutions, by the order of that body, will now be presented to the court

by the Hon. Augustus Brandegee ; and I respectfully request that
the same be entered upon its records, in perpetual testimony of the
regard and affection which its members entertain for the memory
of the deceased."

THE RESOLUTIONS.

At this point Mr. Brandegee rose, and read the following pre-
amble and resolutions : —

" *Whereas*, The Hon. Lafayette S. Foster, a member of the New London County bar and lately a judge of the Supreme Court of this State, has
recently been removed by death : and

" *Whereas*, The members of this bar wish to leave some record of their
high appreciation of his character and worth ; therefore,

" *Resolved*, That he was esteemed by us, as a lawyer, honorable and true,
never betraying a trust ; as an advocate, pre-eminently successful ; as a
senator, ever loyal to the government, clearly discerning what was best
adapted to its interests, and fearlessly giving his influence for their promotion ; as a judge, dignified and uncompromising in the defence of justice
and the right ; as a citizen, ever to be trusted for his integrity and benevolence ; as a friend of universal education, never reluctant to contribute the
wisdom of his counsels and his substance for its diffusion ; as a consistent
representative of the Christian religion, and as a rare model of the virtues
that distinguish a great and good man.

" *Resolved*, That we mourn the extinction of such a light in the private
and official relations of life.

" *Resolved*, That the court be requested to order these resolutions to be
entered upon its minutes, and that the clerk of the bar transmit a copy
thereof to the family of the deceased, and furnish a like copy for publica-
tion in the newspapers of this county."

After the reading of the resolutions Mr. Wait continued as follows : —

ADDRESS OF MR. WAIT.

" Death has again invaded the ranks of our profession, and taken
from us one of our number, who, for many years, has not only been
the acknowledged head of the bar in this county, but occupied a
conspicuous position among the leading practitioners at the bar
of this State.

"The Hon. Lafayette S. Foster, our associate and our friend, has been suddenly struck down by a fatal disease, full of years indeed and crowned with honors, but still in the midst of his usefulness, with his physical powers unshaken, and his intellect unclouded. In this county, in which he was born and passed his entire life, except when temporarily absent in the discharge of public duties, where his character was best understood and his great abilities and many virtues most highly appreciated, his loss as a public man, a personal friend, and a professional brother, is painfully felt and deeply lamented.

"I can but keenly feel the death of one who has not only been my cotemporary and companion in my career at the bar and in public life, but was my friend and associate before I completed the preparation necessary for the pursuit of my profession, and with whom, from the day on which we first met until the hour when he was removed by death, I maintained the most intimate and agreeable relations. * * *

"When I first became acquainted with Mr. Foster, he was a student in the office of the Hon. Calvin Goddard in Norwich; and I was pursuing studies preparatory to entering Washington, now Trinity College, at Hartford. The last few months in which I was so engaged, I recited in the classics to him, and enjoyed very great advantages in having him as my teacher; for he had just graduated, as I have said, from Brown University, with the highest honors of that institution, and was a ripe scholar and admirable instructor. On my leaving college, I at once entered the law office of Mr. Foster, and remained with him as a student — with the exception of a short period during which I pursued the study of law with the Hon. Jabez W. Huntington — until such time as I was admitted to the bar. I allude to my personal relations with the deceased to show the excellent opportunities that I enjoyed to thoroughly know him, and which now enable me to bear pleasant testimony to his nice sense of honor, his unsullied private character, his rare intellectual endowments, and his many and varied accomplishments.

"Ardent and aspiring, he had decided at an early age to pursue the profession of law. Animated by an honorable ambition, deter-

minèd to succeed in this controlling purpose, confident in his own
ability to overcome all ordinary obstacles, from means principally
obtained by teaching, supplemented by such pecuniary aid as a
devoted mother could render, Mr. Foster qualified himself to enter
and sustained himself through college, and acquired his profession.
At the November term of the county court, 1831, he was admitted
to the bar of this county, and at once commenced to practise in
the courts. The early friends of Mr. Foster will recollect that he
attracted attention at that time as a young man of unusual promise, and his future prominence as a jurist and advocate was then
anticipated. At the time that he commenced practice, the bar of
this county presented an array of gifted men who had already won
distinction. Goddard, Strong, Child and Rockwell at Norwich,
Law, Isham, Brainard, Perkins and the younger Cleveland at New
London, Waite and McCurdy at Lyme, were the recognized
leaders, and were formidable competitors of the young aspirant for
professional honors. But, though the task was arduous and the
struggle severe, it was not many years before Mr. Foster succeeded in winning a high reputation as a lawyer. He had been a
close student, not only when preparing for admission to the bar,
but also in the early years after he was admitted, when he had
leisure to familiarize himself with the principles of the common
law, the statutes of our State, and the practice of the courts; so
that when he was subsequently called to the trial of important
causes, he realized the fruits of this course of study, and was prepared to successfully contend with men who enjoyed the advantages of a larger experience and longer established reputations.
Mr. Foster's exertions to take a high rank in his profession and
obtain a lucrative practice were soon crowned with success. His
retainers rapidly increased, his engagements multiplied, litigants
that appreciated his great ability eagerly sought his services, and
not only his rise at the bar of this county but at that of the State
was marked and rapid. He was soon enrolled in the highest rank
of counsellors and advocates. Even when in the full enjoyment of
public honors, he clung to his profession. On his retirement from
the Senate he returned to that pursuit to which he had devoted his

early life, and of late years has been often engaged in the trial of important causes. In the argument of cases, Mr. Foster's manner was easy and impressive, his voice was clear and well modulated. He had a wonderful command of language, an adroitness in grouping the telling facts developed by the testimony, and a forcible mode of presenting the same, that had a potent effect on the court or the jury. All through his long and brilliant professional career, he so conducted as to win the respect of his associates at the bar, and to lead the public to place unlimited confidence in his professional honor and integrity.

"The bench and bar of this State will profoundly feel the great loss that they have met with by the death of Mr. Foster. By his brethren in this county will it be the most deeply appreciated; for they have ever found him in his daily walk a pleasant associate, in forensic struggles an honorable opponent, and, when connected with him in the transaction of business and relying upon his advice and assistance, an able, faithful, and efficient adviser and friend. In his own professional conduct he has ever presented a high standard of honor, integrity, and courtesy, and sought in every way to impart propriety and dignity to the practice of law. May we all ever hold in memory the noble qualities of the great man that has left us, and resolve to pattern after his admirable example!

"It was not as a lawyer of rare ability only that Mr. Foster at an early age became favorably known to the public and won merited distinction. While engaged in the study of the law he took a deep interest in public affairs, and immediately after entering his profession connected himself with the national Republican, and subsequently with the Whig and present Republican, parties. He loved his profession, but at the same time he had a laudable ambition to take a prominent part in the exciting and arduous duties of public life. His political friends in Norwich felt, if he would consent to enter the General Assembly of the State, that they would have in him a faithful and efficient representative, and his party an able and reliable champion. He was many times elected a member of that body, — from 1839 to 1854, — and was three times chosen Speaker of the House. He entered that service in the freshness of his youth, and he was called from it to a higher and broader field of public duty in the maturity of his manhood. He had remarkable gifts for a successful performance of the duties of the Speakership. He was quick, self-possessed, firm of purpose, had an iron control over his temper, and thoroughly understood those parliamentary rules that clothed him with authority and commanded the obedience of the House. Each time that he retired from the Speaker's chair, the members of the House, without distinction of party, bore ample testimony to the ability, courtesy, and impartiality that he displayed as its presiding officer.

" In 1855 Mr. Foster entered the Senate of the United States and remained a member of that body twelve years. He was elected its president *pro tempore* in 1865, and held the position until his retirement from the Senate in 1867. After the assassination of Mr. Lincoln and the advancement of Mr. Johnson to the presidency, he became the acting Vice-President of the United States, and held that high office while he remained a member of the Senate. As the presiding officer of the Senate he maintained the same reputation for great ability that he had earned as Speaker of the Connecticut House of Representatives, and, by blandness of language, firmness of purpose, and personal dignity, commanded the respect and won the esteem of the members of that body.

" While Mr. Foster was connected with the Senate, it numbered among its members some of the most illustrious statesmen that this Republic has ever produced. Fessenden of Maine, Foote and Collamer of Vermont, Anthony of Rhode Island, Seward of New York, Trumbull and Douglass of Illinois, Sumner and Wilson of Massachusetts, Sherman and Wade of Ohio, Grimes of Iowa, Breckenridge and Davis of Kentucky, Saulsbury of Delaware, McDougall of California, Hunter of Virginia, Benjamin of Louisiana, and Frelinghuysen of New Jersey, were among his intimate senatorial associates.

" As a scholar, a lawyer, and a statesman, Mr. Foster ranked among the most distinguished members of the Senate ; and the record that he made, during the twelve years that he was a member of that body, is one of which the State that honored him by placing him there may well be proud. When he first took his seat in the Senate, the slavery question, which had long and violently agitated the country, had nearly reached its culmination. Mr. Foster united with his associate senators from the Northern States in resisting the arrogant demands of the slave power, and by voice and vote sustained the doctrine of human freedom, and the equality of all men before the law. In the great struggle to save the life of the nation and to preserve our free institutions for posterity, from the day when the first Southern State attempted to secede from the Union till the final surrender of the rebel leaders at Appomattox, he took no hesitating nor uncertain part. All his declarations and acts, in the national council or at home, were such as loyalty inspired and love of country demanded.

"In 1870 the town of Norwich again sent Mr. Foster to the Legislature of the State. He was once more chosen Speaker ; and, before the close of the session, he was elected a judge of the Supreme Court, a position which he filled until 1876, when, having reached seventy years of age, he was disqualified by a provision of the Constitution. As a member of the court, Mr. Foster so conducted as to win favorable opinions from lawyers and litigants. His courteous manner to counsel, the patient attention which he exhibited in the trial of causes, his dignified demeanor on the bench, and the strict impartiality and unbending integrity that governed him in his decisions, led the people of the State to hold him in high estimation. His opinions, which he gave as a judge of the court of last resort, and are contained in the recently published volumes of our State reports, disclose extensive research, great legal acquirements, and a clear, active, and well-balanced intellect.

"Other honors were at different times bestowed upon Mr. Foster. He was twice elected mayor of the city of Norwich ; twice he was the candidate of his party for the office of governor of the State ; and in 1851 his *Alma Mater* conferred upon him the honorary degree of Doctor of Laws, a distinction eminently due to his well-known attainments as a scholar as well as a jurist.

"The friends of Mr. Foster who knew him intimately can bear testimony to the versatility of his genius, his untiring industry in the pursuit of knowledge of every kind, and his familiarity with ancient and modern history and English and American literature. His mind was a storehouse of interesting and valuable information; and his fertile imagination, great command of language, and easy utterance, made him a most interesting and instructive companion.

"Mr. Foster was twice married, first to Joanna Boylston Lanman, daughter of Hon. James Lanman, a judge of the Supreme Court of the State and United States senator, and the second time to Martha P. Lyman, daughter of Hon. Jonathan H. Lyman of Northampton, Mass., a prominent lawyer of his day in that State, who died young. His first wife died in 1859; his second survives him. Those of us who through his married life have seen him in his home, can truly say that he was beloved beyond expression in the family circle, and that his house was the abode of generous hospitality and of unalloyed domestic happiness.

"Had I time, I would be glad to allude to other admirable traits in the character of the deceased which he exhibited through life, and which shone with increased lustre as that life drew near its close. But I feel that I have already too long occupied the attention of the court. I will close my imperfect remarks by saying that my brothers of the bar unite with me in the desire to bear public testimony to the worth and virtues of the Hon. Lafayette S. Foster, and that the resolutions which have been presented to the court are the heartfelt expression of their regard and affection for the lamented dead."

REMARKS BY JUDGE PARK.

Judge Park took the resolutions, and said, —

"The court heartily indorses the sentiments so beautifully and graphically expressed in the resolutions of the bar that have been presented regarding the death of the late Judge Foster of this county, and cordially concurs in all the remarks that have been made respecting the same.

"It has been my good fortune to know Judge Foster quite intimately for many years, and it can be truly said that he was worthy of the eulogies that have been bestowed upon his talents and virtues. He possessed great abilities, both natural and acquired, and had in a remarkable degree all those sterling qualities that go to make up an estimable character. To his great learning, legal, scientific, and literary, he added those accomplishments of mind and manner that fitted him to shine in private life, as well as at the bar, on the rostrum, and in the halls of Congress. In his death, he has bequeathed to all the living a notable, pure, and Christian example, commanding universal respect, admiration, and emulation. And in his demise, also, we are all again admonished that 'in the midst of life we are in death.' A few days ago Judge Foster traversed our streets in all the vigor of his early manhood, both mental and physical; now all that remains of this great and good man is the remembrance of his abilities and virtues. Truly is it said that 'death is no respecter of persons.' He strikes alike in cabin, cottage, mansion, and palace. No age, constitution, or position in society is exempt from his ravages. He comes to the high and the low, the rich and the poor, without discrimination. He has visited the court very often in the last few years. Not a judge remains, of either court, except myself, who was there when I had the honor to become a member ; and nearly all have been removed by death.

"Let us all be admonished in time, for the grim monster may appear at our door in a day and an hour that we look not for his coming.

"Mr. Clerk, let the resolutions be entered at length on the records of the court."

V.

MR. FOSTER AS A LAWYER IN 1852.

[From "Sketches of Eminent Americans."]

As a lawyer, Mr. Foster stands in the front rank of his profession in his native State. He is now in the prime of life, in the full vigor and strength of his mental powers, and in the enjoyment of unimpaired health. Mr. Foster, in the commencement of his legal studies, made a thorough elementary preparation ; and, having a retentive and disciplined memory, combined with a brilliant quickness or readiness of manner, he is enabled to make instantly available all his learning and experience. It was in a great measure owing to these circumstances that he was enabled so soon to attain a commanding position in the profession. He excels, both as an advocate and as a counsellor ; and it is that happy union and blending of all the qualities necessary to a good practitioner, that has made him so successful in his profession.

His style of speaking is classic and severe, distinguished by power of argument, appositeness of illustration, and close, logical demonstration. One of its most striking features consists in the entire sincerity with which he argues his cause, leaving no doubt on the minds of his auditory as to his own belief of the truth of what he is saying. His elocution is good, although the intonation of his voice is somewhat sharp.

Having a fine command of the purest English, and a knowledge of its weight and value seldom attained, he is enabled to make his argumentative efforts the more effective from the precision and perspicuity with which they are rendered. This makes him powerful in arguing intricate points of law before a court. When addressing a jury, he manages to fix the attention of the jurors at the outset, before going into the merits of the case, and steadily retains it unbroken to the end. His manner is perfectly self-possessed, his language is in the purest taste, and his arguments are embellished with those graces of oratory which indicate the finished scholar and accomplished lawyer. He is thus enabled, in a double manner, to influence a jury, both by the power of argument and the swaying force of eloquence. In the examination and cross-examination of witnesses, by reason of his strong powers of investigation, he is peculiarly effective, and displays a rare knowledge of human nature. The fast witness he checks, the timid witness he encourages, the reluctant witness he draws out, and the lying witness he so tangles in the mazes of his own falsehoods that he strengthens the very cause he undertook to injure.

He must needs be a skilful and well-disciplined liar who can come unscathed and unexposed from one of Mr. Foster's cross-examinations.

Mr. Foster's highest ambition has been to excel in the line of his profession, to attain a thorough understanding and mastery of legal science; and to this end, with a singleness of purpose, he has directed the untiring industry and energies of a lifetime.

Shrewd and keen, ever on the look-out to detect the weak points of an adversary's position if open to ridicule, his ready exposure of the weakness frequently gives a force and influence favorable to his cause beyond the power of the severest logic or closest reasoning. He possesses the highest powers of wit, together with a keen sense of the ridiculous; and his retorts, on occasions suitable for displaying those powers, are unanswerable. Another marked feature in the professional career of Mr. Foster is his faithfulness and untiring devotion to the interests of his clients. No matter how trifling the amount or how uncertain the prospect of remuneration for his services, he works just as hard and with the same zeal as though the case involved large interests and abundant reward. His practice is very large, extending regularly through all the eastern counties in Connecticut, and to a considerable extent in other portions of the State. * * *

Mr. Foster commenced life with only that inheritance and resource, so often the sole dependence of a New England boy, viz., himself. By a life of strict integrity, laborious study, energetic action, and devotion to the duties and business of the profession he assumed, he has raised himself to rank among the foremost in his native State. Beloved with a fervent warmth of attachment by all who know him personally, and respected by all men of all parties, he stands now, just in the prime of life, at the head of his profession in the eastern part of the State, and the acknowledged leader of his party. In the coming future there are no honors to which he may not aspire, and no place which he would not fill with dignity and honor to himself and credit to his state and country.

VI.

NEW LONDON COUNTY HISTORICAL SOCIETY.

FROM the secretary's annual report of this society, in November, 1880, the following is quoted : —

" For the first time since the organization of this society, at its annual meeting, it has become the sad duty to record in my report a breach so wide as has been made by the loss of one of its most beloved and highly esteemed officers, — our late honored and lamented president. Hon. Lafayette S. Foster, with the late Hon. Henry P. Haven, were among the first to give life to the society. He was one of its most active and efficient friends and counsellors. For nine successive years he had served and honored the society as its president, and always with rare ability and fidelity. At every annual meeting of the society he has been present, presiding with a grace and dignity peculiar to himself, always with words of wise counsel and encouragement. To-day we miss his face, and no longer hear his kind words of sympathy and encouragement. We shall know him no more in this life. His place will be filled by another, but his memory will long be fondly cherished by surviving members. May his falling mantle rest on his successor."

NEW LONDON, CONN., Wednesday, Sept. 22, 1880.

THE adjourned meeting of the New London County Historical Society, held this morning, was presided over by Mr. Daniel Lee. The committee appointed to prepare a notice of the late president of the society, Judge Foster, presented, through the Hon. Benjamin Stark, the chairman, the following memorial record : —

" Lafayette Sabin Foster closed a long and useful life at his home in Norwich on Sunday morning at four o'clock. He was seventy-three years of age. A native of New London County, he took a deep and lively interest in all the objects of our historical society, and was its first president. A graduate of Brown University, he received its highest honor, the degree of doctor of laws. A member of the Legislature of his native State, he was Speaker of the House for three years. A member of the bar of this county, he became a professor of laws in Yale College, and a judge of the Supreme Court of the State. A senator in Congress twelve years, he was president of the Senate and acting Vice-President of the United States for three years. He was successful, and deserved success. In every public station to which he was called, he advanced to its highest position. Such distinguished men are to be remembered for their exemplary aspirations, for their honorable usefulness, and for their fidelity in the discharge of duty. They live in the affection and respect of the people after they have passed away.

"It is eminently proper that the New London County Historical Society should spread upon its minutes a sincere expression of sorrow at the loss it sustains by the demise of its president, and profound acknowledgment of his ardent and uniform devotion to the work of historical research, investigation, and record, for which the society is established.

> "BENJAMIN STARK,
> J. P. C. MATHER,
> J. GEORGE HARRIS,
> F. N. BRAMAN,
> *Committee.*

At the annual meeting of the New London County Historical Society, Feb. 22, 1881, the president, Hon. David A. Wells, elected to fill the vacancy occasioned by the death of Mr. Foster, thus referred ~~in his annual address~~ to his predecessor in office : —

"Although this society, at a previous and specially called meeting, has officially and appropriately noticed the death of our late president, the Hon. Lafayette S. Foster, I am not willing that this our first annual meeting since his decease, should pass without some further reference to this sad event, and without improving the opportunity to ask your attention to the character of the man whom we have known so familiarly, and with whom we have so long been so pleasantly associated.

"There are some lives, which, from their gentleness and even tenor, seem to require to have the seal of death affixed to them in order to fully reveal their characteristics, and enable the world to clearly estimate the extent and sphere of their influence. Such was especially true of our late friend and associate, whose loss we lament, and whose memory we would honor. He was a man whose distinguishing characteristic, more marked, it seems to me, than in any other person I have ever known, was a profound and abiding sense of the obligation of duty incumbent upon him, in common with all others, to the state of which he was a citizen, and to the society of which he was a member; and as he held this sphere of duty and responsibility to be commensurate with the ability of every individual to be good and to do good, and as in his particular case the measure of ability was large, the task which he accordingly imposed upon himself was of necessity of no little magnitude, and came to be an essential element of his every-day life and character. As a consequence of this, he was a man who was always ready, and never waited to be urged, to lend his aid and heartily co-operate with whatever of plan or action promised to benefit either state or society. And yet so modest and unobtrusive was he in all his actions, so devoid was he of every thing in the nature of self-ostentation, so noiselessly did he come and go amongst us, doing faithfully the many things which his hands found to do, that society in a measure failed, while he lived, to recognize as it should the daily beauty of his life, or the excellence of the example which, in every position to which he was called, he continually exhibited to those about him. His life indeed resembled one of those powerful and well-adjusted pieces of mechanism, which perform their work so quietly, and yet so effectively, that it is not easy to realize the force that they transmit, or that they have any intimate connection with the striking results of the more showy and noisy machinery by which they are surrounded. But now that he has gone, and now that we seek to find others who shall fitly stand in his place and assume his trusts, we recognize, by the difficulty of finding them, how exceptional were his qualities, how beneficial was his influence, and how great a loss society has sustained in his death, at a ripe and full, but nevertheless at an untimely age, because 'his eye was not dim nor his natural force abated.'

"To Mr. Foster this society owes a large debt of gratitude. He needed no solicitation to take an active part in its inception and management, because he saw that the work which the society proposed to itself to do was useful, that it would contribute to keep alive the memories of our fathers, and strengthen their sons, through those memories, in those kindly relations which especially spring from a feeling of a common ancestry and heritage ; and although at our annual gatherings few might be present, his place was never vacant.

"With temperaments and organizations so various that no two of the individuals that make up the generations of men are said to be in all respects alike, the judgments which we personally form respecting our fellow men must necessarily be different and often conflicting ; but I feel confident that you will agree with me that the attributes which I have ascribed to Mr. Foster were those which especially characterized him, and that he was, by reason of them, in all respects a model citizen. And if to this designation I were to add any thing more of deserved and not fulsome praise, I should say that he was pre-eminently a pure man ; one who had girt himself about with such a sense of personal honor and self-respect, that meanness and selfishness shrunk abashed and retreated in his presence ; a man who had such self-control, that, if under a sense of personal wrong the harsh word perchance rose to his lips, it was rarely or never uttered ; and who, without malice to any, had an unbounded charity for all. And if the New London County Historical Society do no more than enshrine and perpetuate the memory of its first president, Lafayette S. Foster, its mission certainly will not have been in vain."

VII.

NORWICH FREE ACADEMY.

AT a meeting of the Trustees of the *Norwich Free Academy*, held Sept. 20, 1880, the Board passed the following resolutions, and adjourned : —

" *Whereas*, by the Providence of Almighty God, Hon. L. F. S. Foster, one of this Board of Trustees, has been removed by death.

"Therefore, *Resolved*, That in the death of Hon. L. F. S. Foster we have lost one of the original corporators of this institution. Elected a trustee in September, 1859, he has always manifested a strong interest in the cause of education in this city, and by his advice and contributions made his influence felt.

" To his family we offer our sympathy, and will, as a Board of Trustees, attend his funeral, and publish this resolution in ' The Morning Bulletin.' "

VIII.

HON. LAFAYETTE S. FOSTER, LL.D.

[From the "Bible Society Record," November, 1880.]

THE Board of Managers having received the announcement of the decease of the Hon. Lafayette S. Foster, LL.D., recently a vice-president of the American Bible Society, place upon their Minutes this tribute to his memory : —

" Mr. Foster died at his home in Norwich, Conn., after a brief illness, on Sunday, Sept. 19th, 1880, in the seventy-fourth year of his age. A native of New London County, he graduated with the highest honors of his class at Brown University, in 1828, and after a course of legal study was admitted to the bar in Norwich, in 1831. His public career from that time onward is one to which his friends point with peculiar satisfaction. For ten successive years he was sent to the State Legislature, and was repeatedly chosen Speaker of the lower House. For two full terms he was a member of the United States Senate; and during part of that time, after the death of Mr. Lincoln, he was acting Vice-President of the United States. In 1868 he was chosen Professor of Law in Yale College; and in 1870 he was elected judge of the Supreme Court of Connecticut, serving in that capacity until he reached the 'age of threescore years and ten.

"While Mr. Foster filled these various positions in public life with conspicuous ability, he was also most highly esteemed in private life and in the Christian church. His official relation to this Board began with his election as vice-president in 1878; but, for years before, he had been a life member of the society, and had interested himself in its work.

"The Board of Managers deeply regret the loss which they have sustained in the decease of this honored and eminent associate, whose sympathy and counsels they had hoped to share for years to come."

IX.

CONNECTICUT PRISON ASSOCIATION.

IN the annual report of the Connecticut Prison Association, submitted to the Legislature of 1880–81, the Hon. Francis Wayland, chairman of the executive committee of the association, pays the following tribute to the services of the late Hon. Lafayette S. Foster to the cause of prison reform: —

"Since our last report, the Association has suffered a serious loss in the death of Hon. Lafayette S. Foster, long one of its vice-presidents and a member of its executive committee. Although the numerous engagements of Mr. Foster prevented his regular attendance at our quarterly meetings, he never failed to give us the benefit of his counsels and the support of his encouraging words. Those who knew Judge Foster will not be surprised to learn that the condition of the discharged prisoner, homeless and friendless, but sincerely desiring to earn an honest livelihood, strongly appealed to his warm heart and his well-informed philanthropy. His views of the duty which society and the state owe to this most unfortunate class were clearly defined, and always on the side of enlightened humanity. Too wise to waste his sympathy in sentimental regrets, he labored with his fellow officers of the Prison Association to devise the best means to help the prisoner by teaching him to help himself. As might have been expected from the character of the man, his suggestions, founded on long experience at the bar and on the bench, were thoroughly practical and conservative. What he had seen of the causes of crime, the temptations by which weak or ignorant men are assailed, of the criminal instinct which is inherited, and of the evil companionship which is demoralizing, had taught him that, while violations of law must be punished for the protection of society, no pains should be spared to make such punishment tend towards the reformation of the offender. He deprecated undue severity in prison regulations, and considered it of prime importance that all the influences surrounding the convict should be of such a nature as to insure the best possible preparation for a reformed life. Believing that the moment of the prisoner's discharge is a crisis in his career, and that judicious efforts made in his behalf at this time, may, in many cases, reclaim him from the ranks of crime, he was among the first to approve the formation of this Association, and became at once one of its most useful officers. His memory will be held in the highest esteem by those to whom he gave such cordial and intelligent support, and who ever found him an efficient ally in the cause of prison reform."

X.

EXTRACT FROM THE ANNUAL REPORT OF PRESIDENT
PORTER TO THE FELLOWS OF YALE COLLEGE,
OCTOBER, 1880.

THE Hon. Lafayette S. Foster, recently deceased, has made provision in his will for a legacy of sixty thousand dollars, to be paid at some future day for the endowment of a Professorship of Common Law. This very generous gift is valuable not alone for the direct benefit which it will bring to the school. It is also the fulfilment of a long-cherished hope that some member of the legal profession would provide in this way for the specific object of instruction in its principles and its practice, by securing to the teacher that comparative exemption from many of the duties and cares that are incident to active and laborious practice which seems to be essential to the highest success. The principle has long been recognized among liberal minds, that every man is in many senses "a debtor to his profession." The obligations which are so generally acknowledged are various. It is not often possible that a single individual should at the same time be able and disposed to discharge them by founding a professorship for legal instruction. The memory of our late eminent judge, senator, practitioner, and teacher will long be honored in this institution for this liberal and sagacious benefaction.

XI.

WE forbear annexing other obituary notices which appeared in the various public journals; but the following extracts, from a few of the many private letters received after Mr. Foster's death, attest the love and confidence that his life inspired, and the wide sense of bereavement which his death occasioned.

From Dr. James C. Welling.

* * * "I feel that I must reach out my hand to you in simple token of the share I would take in this affliction which has not only come to darken your home and desolate your heart, but also has come to carry grief into a thousand homes and hearts within which the name of your husband was cherished with esteem and with affection.

"Having been honored with his friendship in other days, I can bear my humble testimony to the high intellectual qualities, the sterling goodness, and the lovely social graces which endeared him to all with whom he was brought into intimate relations ; and from the sadness which fills my heart, now that I shall see him no more, I can readily measure the sense of loss which must oppress the bosom of those who loved him most because they knew him best.

"In a moment like this, I may not venture to mock your sorrow with words of consolation; only there *is* consolation in the review of a life which was noble and pure in all its impulses, and to which the hand of death has now set the seal of a sacred consecration." * * *

From Hon. E. W. Stoughton.

* * * "I well know how utterly unavailing is the effort of friends to diminish anguish like yours by any attempt at consolation. I know, however, that to one so bereaved, comfort may be found in the consciousness that the husband you mourn was honored as statesman and patriot by millions of his countrymen, and beloved by many, very many friends, among whom I count myself not the least. His qualities of mind and heart, his great abilities never misapplied, his high cultivation and thorough breeding, always harmonizing with the simplicity of noblest manhood, made him the

favorite of all who knew him, and a standard for men to imitate. To have lived as he did, in the most tragic period of our national life, to have been a marked and noble actor in that tragedy, to have passed through it honored by all, even by those he opposed as the enemies of his country, was a career which will glorify the grave where he is to rest, and must cause even your sad heart to beat with sacred pride and solemn joy at the thought that its love was to him dearer than all his earthly honors." * * *

From Professor Simeon E. Baldwin.

NEW HAVEN, October, 1880.

* * * "An acquaintance which began at my father's house in my childhood had ripened into a real friendship. Few men of his age have kept so freshly the warm feelings of youth, or been so fully in sympathy with the changes of modern thought, and whatever belongs to genuine reform. He has been as active and successful in the public service since leaving the bench as he was before, and the history of his life shows no break up to the end." * * *

From Hon. Robert C. Winthrop.

BROOKLINE, MASS., Sept. 20, 1880.

* * * "Among the men whom I have known in public and in private life, there was no one left for whom I had a higher regard or a warmer respect than for your lamented husband. The announcement of his death gave me real grief. I had anticipated for him many more years of useful and honorable life, and had hoped, that, in the retirement which age had brought to us both, I might more frequently enjoy the privilege of his society. God has ordered it otherwise ; and it is only for us who remain to cherish the memory of his excellence." * * *

From Mr. J. L. Penniman.

PHILADELPHIA, December, 1880.

* * * "Every one must testify to Mr. Foster's earnestness and purity of purpose, to his generosity and benevolence of life, to the warm and affectionate attachments of his heart, to his love for and devotion to all the truths of our holy Christian religion, to his marked intellectuality, all of which were fully and freely dedicated to his God, his country, and his friends." * * *

From Gen. George W. Cullum.

NEW YORK, Sept. 23, 1880.

* * * "As a statesman and jurist, it is unnecessary that I should speak of your husband, for the whole country has already resounded with appreciative eulogies and just praises; but, as my personal friend, I grieve for his loss almost as for a brother, for I had known him more than a quarter of a century, and with each revolving year I more and more appreciated his purity of heart, his manly virtues, his nobility of nature, his steadfast loyalty to country and friends, and all his sweet, refined, and graceful amenities which captivated the affections of all his social circle. Little did I think, when I last sat at his side at Mr. Stoughton's dinner, that his genial spirit, his sparkling wit, his exuberant humor, his wealth of culture, and all his polished courtesies, marking the true gentleman, I should enjoy no more forever. A great man and a brave spirit has gone; and I feel a wide gap left in my heart, for I truly loved him." * * *

From President Gilman.

JOHNS HOPKINS UNIVERSITY, BALTIMORE,
Sept. 25, 1880.

* * * "I hope you will not deem it intrusive if I give expression in this way to the affection and respect I have long felt for your

honored husband, who met us so cordially a few weeks ago within your doors, and promised, if possible, to come and see us again next winter. From my earliest recollection he has been a representative man, not only in Norwich, but in Connecticut, and before the entire nation ; and throughout a long, unsullied political career he has been an example of enlightened, independent, and patriotic statesmanship. There are few public men who have gone through the changes of the last twenty or thirty years with a record so worthy as his to be honorably and gratefully remembered. Although my personal intercourse with him has been occasional rather than constant, it has, perhaps for this very reason, left a very strong impression on my memory ; and I feel that I have lost a friend whom it was always a pleasure to meet, and whose public and private virtues it will always be a pleasure to recall and honor." * * *

From Rev. Henry A. Miles.

HINGHAM, MASS., Sept. 29, 1880.

* * * " My recollection of your husband runs back long prior to your first knowledge of him. In college he was known for traits of character which have distinguished him through life, — a courtesy of manners which everywhere won friends, a force of will which was not turned aside by obstacles, a power of concentration never satisfied till it had penetrated to the bottom of a subject, and a sportive, joyous nature which poured sunlight around his path. Not often are the words more true that 'the boy is father of the man.' "

From Gen. J. Watts De Peyster.

NEW YORK, September, 1880.

* * * " Mr. Foster's loss is a national one. I was shocked at the sad news. I esteemed him as much as any gentleman with whom I was acquainted. He was beloved and respected by every one who

knew him. He was a universal favorite. It is marvellous how he endeared and impressed himself on every person of ability and standing with whom he came in contact. I have heard gentlemen who rarely give way to enthusiasm warm up to it in remembering the exquisite courtesy and integrity of your husband. * * * From Mr. Foster's appearance and activity I thought I should long enjoy his friendship in this world." * * *

From Hon. Augustus Brandegee.

NEW LONDON, July 15, 1881.

* * * "It was my great privilege to have known Senator Foster since the session of the Connecticut House of Representatives in 1854, of which he was Speaker, and from which he was, during the session, transferred to the Senate of the United States. I was associated with him in public life during the momentous issues of both war and peace which have made the Thirty-Eighth and Thirty-Ninth Congresses historic.

"Upon his return to the practice of the profession of which he was a most conspicuous ornament, I was frequently associated with or against him in the friendly contentions of the bar; and of recent years, in the management of a common trust, I had a rare opportunity of frequent and friendly intercourse.

"With these opportunities for observation and acquaintance, I can safely say, I never knew a man more honorable, more just, more pure and upright. As a senator he was among the foremost when there were giants in that chamber. He was a trusted counsellor of Lincoln, and respected and beloved by his associates. As a judge he was conscientious, dignified, learned, and impartial. As a lawyer he was unsurpassed. He had every qualification which was needed to maintain a position in the front rank, whether as an advocate before the jury or the judges. In learning, eloquence, pathos, wit, argument, sarcasm, and tact, — all brought to contribute towards the highest success in the noblest of professions, — he was *facile princeps*.

"It was not till the later years, when admitted to a closer acquaintance and more friendly intercourse, that I came to know and appreciate the sweeter and more lovable traits of his character which the grave and dignified manner of his bearing at first somewhat concealed. He was as full of tenderness and sympathy as a woman. He was replete with humor and anecdote, — genial, cheerful, and scrupulously careful of not only the rights but the feelings and even the sensitiveness of others.

"As his sun began to descend toward the west, it lost none of its meridian glory ; but it took on a mellower and softer radiance, and cast its level and genial beams on all that surrounded it. He was not only a great, but he was a good, man. And when he died without the first cloud upon his faculties, or the first stain upon his fame, he was to my mind, whether for the spotlessness of his character, the abilities he possessed, or the honors he had enjoyed, — The first Citizen of Connecticut." * * *

From Professor Edwards A. Park.

ANDOVER, MASS., Sept. 28, 1880.

* * * "I cannot tell you how much I was appalled by hearing of the affliction which has come upon you. * * * I became acquainted with Mr. Foster fifty-six years ago. We were college mates, but not classmates. He was distinguished for his ready and retentive memory, — it was wonderful ; and for his sprightly wit, — that also was remarkable. He held a high rank as a scholar. No one of his fellow students surpassed him. In all respects his character was above reproach. I anticipated his future eminence. In 1839 I met him in Washington, and was delighted to notice his moral as well as intellectual progress. I called with him on President Van Buren. He seemed to be at home in the society of the President and his cabinet. He appeared to be evidently designed for a high position in the Congress of the United States, and for performing a good and great service there. When a student in college I anticipated for him a distinguished career as a statesman. After he had

finished that career I met him occasionally at our *Alma Mater*, and was charmed with his cordial manners and exuberance of social feeling, — in fact with all the characteristics which I admired in him while we were fellow students. He was always ready to introduce religious topics into his familiar converse with me. His mind was apt to dwell on things unseen and eternal. I saw convincing proof that he had retained his fealty to his conscience throughout his public career. I had esteemed him as a great man ; and the more intimately I knew him, more and more did I esteem him as a good man. He did not obtrude his religious principles upon the public, but he cherished them in the sanctuary of his own soul. * * * I cannot easily bring myself to believe that I shall never see him again, for when I last met him he appeared to be a picture of health and vitality." * * *

XII.

CONCERNING THE DIGNITY OF A RETIRED PUBLIC OFFICER.[1]

[From "The New York Independent."]

On the foregoing subject, which has occupied the ingenious solicitude of so many eminent contributors to " The Independent," it would not be becoming in me to venture with mere expressions of my own opinion. But, having been personal witness of a very eminent example exactly bearing on the question under consideration, I am bold to believe that a statement of it may be as well worth pondering as the arguments and opinions even of the most illustrious of your correspondents.

The church which it is my privilege to serve in the Gospel has been most sorely bereaved, within a few months, by the death of beloved and venerated members, and notably by the death of La-

---

[1] Written on some one's proposal, seriously discussed, to endow retired Presidents and Vice-Presidents of the United States with large pensions, and with life membership in the Senate.

fayette S. Foster, who for the twelve most momentous years of American history was a Senator of the United States, and for a part of that time was President of the Senate, and, after the death of President Lincoln and the accession of Mr. Johnson to the Presidency, succeeded to the chair of Vice-President. Until the expiration of his senatorial term he fulfilled the duties of this high position with a dignity, a fine courtesy, and a commanding ability which I have often heard spoken of by public men, but never spoken of except with admiration. The greatness of his public services during those memorable years is not at all to be measured by his official station or his public acts. Few men were more resorted to for private personal counsel by Abraham Lincoln — as, one after another, or many at a time, the awful questions of the war emerged — than the upright, clear-headed, learned senator from Connecticut; and in the hardly less stormy days of reconstruction, when great measures were pending, there was no place where men whose single anxiety was to do the best thing for the whole country were more apt to find each other in private conference than at Senator Foster's apartment. His was a senatorial career to which Connecticut citizens look back with a sense of honorable pride.

From the second position in the Republic Mr. Foster returned, in the ripe strength of his manhood, to his home in Norwich and to the absolute level of private citizenship. No doubt that which is alleged concerning the retiring presidents was true in this case, — that his private business had suffered by his twelve years' devotion to public affairs. Certainly this was true, that the compensations with which some public men manage to balance this drawback were wholly absent in his case. There had been no salary grab in his time; and, if there had been a whiskey ring, that made some senators rich without visible disgrace, he was not in it. He came back to his fellow·citizens, as he went from among them, with "clean hands and a pure heart," and resumed practice as a lawyer. Something had been lost, no doubt, by the long disuse of his profession, — something of facility in practice, something of the "run of business." But more had been gained in solidity of mind, in breadth of character, in a reputation wide as the continent; so that if there would have been difficulty in his taking at once just the same place he had left, there was no difficulty at all in his taking a place higher and more honorable,— I do not say and would not care to say more lucrative.

Those that best knew Mr. Foster and the needs of the public service, grudged that his large and unselfish wisdom, ripened by an experience so long and exceptional, should be lost to the national councils; but it did not occur to them — certainly it did not to him — that there was need of any other way of getting a desirable man into the Senate besides that of electing him to it. He thought it no dishonor, either to himself or to the station he had filled, to serve as a member of the lower house of the Connecticut Legislature, and to accept the Speaker's chair of that unimposing body. For a few years, until retired by law at the age of seventy, he was judge of the Supreme Court of Connecticut, but returned at once from the bench to the bar, of which he was the ornament and pride.

It was in these later years only that I have known him well. That courtly but most genial gentleman, the recollections of whose life were a thrilling chapter of unwritten history, the wit and wisdom of whose table talk gave added charms to his generous hospitality, was, in point of civil station, only a diligent and honorable attorney at law. One other office he held. He was teacher of a Bible class in the Sunday school of the Park Church. This will, doubtless, seem undignified to some of your correspondents; but there are few figures in my memory that I recall with more of reverence than that vigorous form, scarcely beginning to droop under the burden of years, and that " good gray head that all men knew," standing before his class in animated discourse on a chapter of the word of God, or in words of singular grace and reverent beauty leading the prayers of our Thursday evening meeting.

I have been in the habit, these two years that I have been neighbor to Mr. Foster, of looking upon his diligent, fruitful, and honorable old age as presenting the very type and ideal of a worthy close to the career of a great statesman and public official in a Republic such as ours. I have been glad that such an example should be before the eyes of my sons; and, when visitors from the Old World have come to see me, I have taken pride in pointing to the late acting Vice-President of the United States, taking his modest place and work on an equality with all the rest of us, as a noble and characteristic example of what is best in American republicanism.

LEONARD WOOLSEY BACON.

Norwich, Conn., Nov. 29, 1880.

www.ingramcontent.com/pod-product-compliance
Lightning Source LLC
Chambersburg PA
CBHW032008010726
47493CB00007B/2320